DON'T YOU DARE READ THIS, MRS. DUNPHREY

Also by Margaret Peterson Haddix

The Always War
Claim to Fame
Palace of Mirrors
Uprising
Double Identity
The House on the Gulf
Escape from Memory
Takeoffs and Landings
Turnabout
Just Ella
Leaving Fishers

The Missing series
Found
Sent
Sabotaged
Torn
Caught

The Shadow Children series
Among the Hidden
Among the Impostors
Among the Betrayed
Among the Barons
Among the Brave
Among the Enemy
Among the Free

The Girl with 500 Middle Names
Because of Anya
Say What?
Dexter the Tough
Running Out of Time

DON'T YOU DARE READ THIS, MRS. DUNPHREY

Margaret Peterson Haddix

SIMON & SCHUSTER BFYR
An imprint of Simon & Schuster Children's Publishing Division
1230 Avenue of the Americas, New York, New York 10020

This book is a work of fiction. Any references to historical events, real people, or real locales are used fictitiously. Other names, characters, places, and incidents are products of the author's imagination, and any resemblance to actual events or locales or persons, living or dead, is entirely coincidental.
Copyright © 1996 by Margaret Peterson Haddix
All rights reserved, including the right of reproduction in whole or in part in any form.
SIMON & SCHUSTER BFYR is a trademark of Simon & Schuster, Inc.

For information about special discounts for bulk purchases, please contact Simon & Schuster Special Sales at 1-866-506-1949 or business@simonandschuster.com.
The Simon & Schuster Speakers Bureau can bring authors to your live event. For more information or to book an event, contact the Simon & Schuster Speakers Bureau at 1-866-248-3049 or visit our website at www.simonspeakers.com.
Book design by Tom Daly
The text for this book is set in Century Book.
Manufactured in the United States of America
This SIMON & SCHUSTER BFYR paperback edition April 2012
2 4 6 8 10 9 7 5 3 1
The Library of Congress has cataloged the hardcover edition as follows:
Haddix, Margaret Peterson.
Don't you dare read this, Mrs. Dunphrey / Margaret Peterson Haddix. — 1st ed.
p. cm.
Summary: In the journal she is keeping for English class, sixteen-year-old Tish chronicles the changes in her life when her abusive father returns home after a two-year absence.
ISBN 978-0-689-80097-9 (hc)
[1. Child abuse—Fiction. 2. Fathers and daughters—Fiction. 3. Diaries—Fiction.] I. Title.
PZ7.H1164 Do 1996
95-43200
ISBN 978-1-4424-4315-0 (pbk)
ISBN 978-1-4391-1527-5 (eBook)

Acknowledgments

With thanks to Janet Peterson,

Susan Zaffiro, Bob McHale,

and the wards of the state of Indiana

who told me their stories.

DON'T YOU DARE READ THIS,
MRS. DUNPHREY

AUGUST 28

All right, Mrs. Dunphrey, you said we had to do these journals, but if we wanted to write something personal and private we could mark an entry, "Do not read." And then you wouldn't read it, you'd just check to make sure we'd written something. Right? Okay, that's what I want. Don't read the rest of this entry.

Did you stop reading? I can't believe a teacher would be so stupid. That's what Eric Lynch was getting at, when he asked, "So, like, we could mark every single entry, 'Don't read'? And then we could write anything?" Everybody knows that Eric handed in the words to "Row, Row, Row Your Boat," written over and over again, instead of outlines in his history notebook last year. And Mr. Tremont never even noticed, because he doesn't really check anything, even though he says he does. Eric told everyone Mr. Tremont wrote, "Good job. Nice penmanship. A."

And you're telling us you don't check? I can tell you're a first-year teacher, Mrs. Dunphrey.

But what if I do write something personal, and you really are reading these?

I'm going to give you a test. I'm going to write something that's secret, that no one else would know about me, and see if you are reading this. Let's see, the secret is . . . I know how to crochet.

You think that's not such a great secret? Well, you probably haven't figured out whose journal this is. This is Tish Bonner writing. I'm one of the girls who sits in the back row. We all have big hair. Mr. Tremont calls us the gum-cracking brigade. You looked kind of scared when Sandy, Rochelle, Chastity, and I walked into the room today. Let me clue you in: we don't crochet. Crocheting's for old ladies and prissy girls like Heather Turner. You probably haven't met her yet—you'd know her because she's got the flattest hair in the school. It's a little greasy, too. She wants to be a home ec teacher when she grows up. She had a crush on Mr. Tremont last year (Have you met him yet? He's bald and ugly and has a stomach bigger than the globe in his classroom.) and she brought him homemade cookies. Oatmeal. That's Heather Turner. That's not me.

So, you're probably wondering, how is it that I know how to crochet?

Hey, I said one secret. That's it. If I can't trust you—if you are reading this—I can't give too much away.

AUGUST 30

Don't read this, Mrs. Dunphrey.

Do you know what a drag school is? Maybe you really

don't—maybe you liked it when you were a kid. Maybe you think it's fun now. You looked like you were having fun today, or trying to, talking about commas at the board. I mean, commas! Who cares? Don't you have anything more important to worry about?

I do, let me tell you. And I would tell you, but I haven't handed this in yet to see if you pass my test.

School, though. That's what I was talking about. You've got us doing this stupid journal, Mr. Tremont wants another stupid history notebook from us every six weeks, Mrs. Rachethead (oops, sorry—Mrs. Racheau) is going to make us dissect frogs soon, Mr. Steinway gives us three pages of geometry homework every night . . . Who cares? I've got to work at Burger Boy most nights and almost every weekend. If I don't—hey, no clothes, no food, no nothing for Ms. Tish Bonner. Or probably not for Matt Bonner (that's my brother), either. You don't think my mom gives us money, do you?

If it weren't for getting to see my friends at school, I'd probably drop out. Hey—that's another test for you, isn't it? You teachers are programmed to freak whenever someone talks about dropping out. If you really are reading this, I'd be slapped into the dropout prevention program so fast my head would spin. You know what everybody calls the dropout prevention program? Drip prevention. Smart, huh? It gets the drips out of school without them dropping out.

Really, I can't drop out, though. Then what would I do? No laying around the house watching TV for Ms. Tish

Bonner. My mother's already doing that herself. (Ha, ha.) I'd probably have to go to full-time at the Burger Boy. I'd probably be doing that the rest of my life.

And you know what? I really hate the Burger Boy. A lifetime of dishing out burgers and curly fries—no thanks.

SEPTEMBER 1

Don't read this, Mrs. Dunphrey.

You sure you want us to write in these twice a week? My life's not so exciting that I have something to say twice a week. I don't have anything to say at all. But you said we had to have four entries before we handed these in on Friday . . . So, hey, here this is.

I'm writing this in Mr. Tremont's class. He probably thinks I'm taking notes. Except no one else is taking notes, so why would I? It's not like he would expect me to be a standout student.

I'll tell you now: I'm a C student. Sometimes I get B's, when I get lucky. I don't study. One time last year when we were freshmen, they made us take some aptitude test. I don't know what I was thinking, but I really tried hard for once. Guess I just wanted to see what I could do. And you know what? I knocked the socks off everybody. I did better than Susan Stanwick and Mike Hardy, and everybody knows they've got computers where their brains are supposed to be. (After that, Susan went around telling people she was coming down with the flu that day—that's why she didn't have the highest score for the first time in her life. Yeah, right.)

It was too much hassle, though. For about a week, I had all the counselors and teachers swarming all over me. I can still hear Miss Anthony saying, "Now that we all know what you're capable of, Tish, I'm going to expect a lot more out of you . . ." Like I was really going to start doing my algebra homework. Mrs. Herzenberger started talking to me about college. Then it's like everybody remembered what they were dealing with, and forgot me. Hey, I'm not one of those kids who grew up in Chateau Estates or Golf Terrace. I only live four blocks from the school. You've probably been past my house—and if you haven't, you've seen ones just like it. Small. Poor. Falling down. You think there's any money stashed away in some college fund for me? Uh-huh. Right. Tell me another joke.

Have you ever noticed Mr. Tremont says "so to speak" every other sentence? He's doing it now and it's driving me crazy. I'll take down every word he says: "The French and Indian War, so to speak, was part of a much larger event . . . something, something (I can't get this all) and Americans, so to speak, get a little egocentric looking back on this event, so to speak . . ."

Gag, gag, gag.

SEPTEMBER 4

Don't read this, Mrs. Dunphrey.

This is due next period, so I've got to get this done

quickly. Mrs. Rachethead is looking at me . . .

Oops, I couldn't go on because Mrs. Rachethead was really, really suspicious. I guess we were supposed to be taking a test. Now it's two minutes before your class is going to start and I'm trying to write fast, but it doesn't matter because this entry isn't going to be long enough.

Tish,

Except for your fourth entry, you seem to be writing plenty. Please try to keep up the volume. If you make this a regular habit, you'll find it easier and easier to do. Just this once, I'll give you full credit, because your first three entries are long. But try to write long entries every time.

SEPTEMBER 9

Don't read this entry, Mrs. Dunphrey.

So I need to keep up my volume. Yes, ma'am. I hope you didn't write anything like that on any of the boys' journals. They'd make a dirty joke out of it. And they already make enough comments about you, just because you're young and smile a lot. You know, if I foufed up your bangs some, you could pass for one of us.

But anyhow, maybe you can't help writing stupid things on our papers. Maybe it's required, being a teacher and all.

You did pass my test, though. I went up to you after class today, after you'd handed back our journals, and asked, "Do you know how to crochet?" And you looked at me so stupidly I knew you hadn't read that entry in my journal.

I still think you're being dumb, but at least I feel safe now. Safer, anyway.

Because I don't have anything else to write about, I will tell how I learned to crochet. My Granma taught me a long time ago. My Granma's dead now. She died four years ago. After the funeral, I took the afghan she'd been teaching me to crochet and threw it to the back of my closet. I think it's still there, but hidden, under a bunch of old tennis shoes.

This is funny, because I hadn't really thought about crocheting or that afghan in a long time. But lately, sometimes when I'm lying in bed almost asleep or almost awake, my fingers kind of twitch, and I realize they're moving the same way they used to move when I crocheted.

Weird, huh? I'm glad you're not actually reading this. I'm glad no one is. Only—it'd be nice to have someone to talk about things like this with.

SEPTEMBER 11

Don't read this, Mrs. Dunphrey.

I guess I made it sound in my last entry like I didn't have any friends. I do. I have lots, actually. Sandy and Rochelle and Chastity are the best friends anyone could ever have, and then there are lots of other people who at least kind of like me.

Sandy and Rochelle and Chastity and me, we hang out a lot together, on the weekends and after school, when none of us are working. We go up to the mall and find the tightest jeans and shortest skirts. Sandy's been known to shoplift some of the clothes or sometimes just lipstick or eyeshadow at Target. She says the stores expect a certain amount of shoplifting—they build it into the prices. So, really, she's just getting her money's worth if she shoplifts. You'd think she'd know better, since her father's a lawyer. But maybe she figures if she gets caught, he can get her off. Rochelle and Chastity and me, we wouldn't be so lucky. Our dads couldn't help us. (Like, I'd have to find my dad first, even if he could help me.) Maybe that's why we never take anything.

Chastity and Sandy both have boyfriends, and Rochelle's always madly in love with some new guy. They're always wanting to fix me up with someone. I don't know. I usually find some excuse. Usually I have to work. The guys they like, the ones they try to fix me up with, they always have pimples or bad breath, or they say dumb things like, "So, you want to get laid?" when you've just met them. Rochelle says I'm picky. I told her once that she had no standards. She got mad and wouldn't speak to me for three days. Chastity—she's the one who's always making people make up—Chastity finally made us both apologize.

But, really, are there any guys out there who aren't jerks? I don't even know any grown-up men who aren't jerks. My dad was never Mr. Wonderful, not that I ever saw. Who else am I supposed to look up to? Mr. Tremont? (So to speak.)

You must be married, Mrs. Dunphrey, if your name is Mrs.—is your husband a jerk?

SEPTEMBER 13

Don't read this, Mrs. Dunphrey.

It's Sunday afternoon, and I'm going to go crazy if I don't get out of this house. Mom's watching some dumb movie—one of those black and white things from before I was born. She's got it turned up real loud, like that's going to keep Matt and me from knowing she's crying. Only I don't think she's crying about the movie. She'd be crying anyway.

Since my dad left, it's been like Mom's not really here, either. She could be a ghost or a shadow. Now that I think about it, though, she's always been kind of a shadow. When Dad was here, it was whatever Dad wanted, Mom did. I don't know why she misses him. It's not like anyone was happy when he was around.

I remember one winter when I was maybe ten, it was really, really cold. It was Christmastime, and Granma had Matt and me trying to decorate the Christmas tree. (It was just one of those fake silver ones—real ugly.) Dad came home, and he had icicles hanging from his beard, it was that cold. Matt ran up to him and started gibbering about Santa Claus coming and bringing presents—Matt was only two or three then, so he didn't know any better. Anyhow, Dad told him, "Oh Matt, don't you know? It's so cold outside that all Santa's reindeer are going to freeze. No presents this year."

Matt started crying, and Granma took him up on her lap and kept saying, "Ssh, ssh, it's all right. That's not true. Reindeer can stand any kind of weather." The whole time she was glaring at Dad. Dad got mad and started yelling about how Granma thought she knew more about taking care of his kids than he did. He ran outside and Mom ran after him, even though she was just wearing slippers and a robe. No coat. Dad couldn't get the truck to start, and Granma and Matt and me, we could hear the engine turning over and over, and Mom and Dad yelling at each other. And Mom crying.

The weird thing is, I remember that as a happy moment,

because Matt and Granma and me were all cuddled up on the couch together. It was warm in the house, and Mom and Dad yelling was something outside, like the wind, that couldn't get to us. The lights on the silver tree were blinking on and off, all bright and shiny. I thought it was beautiful.

Mom's crying louder now. Those stupid actors in the movie she's watching are talking about true love, like it's something real. I'm going to call Sandy and see if she'll go to the mall with me. Maybe we can take Matt, and he won't have to listen to Mom either.

SEPTEMBER 16

Don't read this entry, Mrs. Dunphrey.

Aren't you proud of me? This isn't due for two days, and I'm doing my last entry already. I wouldn't admit this to anyone, of course, but this journal stuff isn't too bad. It's better than any of the other homework you teachers make us do. As long as you're not reading this, I can just put down whatever I'm thinking.

I'm feeling bad because I had a fight with Matt this morning. Well, not really a fight, but—a problem. I always help him get ready for school, because Mom's working nights now, at Haggarty's SuperValu. Cash register. She doesn't get home until after we're at school, but I'm not sure if that's when she gets off or just when she finally gets around to getting in. Anyhow, this morning, Matt was taking a long time eating his Cheerios. It's like he had to eat each one individually. I told him to hurry up. I didn't mean to be mean, but it came out sounding nasty. like maybe something my dad would say. Matt started gulping down his cereal, and then he picked up his bowl and was going to drink all the leftover milk. Only, he was going too fast, and half the milk spilled down his front.

"Now look what you've done," I said, and this time I really did sound mean. And I didn't care, because I knew that meant he was going to have to change his shirt, and I wasn't sure if he had any clean ones left. There was no way we were going to be able to leave on time.

It would have been okay if Matt had yelled back at me—maybe told me it was my fault for making him hurry. But he just sat there and bent his head down, and I could see his lip trembling. And then these little tears started rolling down his cheeks. His yellow hair was sticking out all over the place, and he had a milk moustache, and he looked totally, totally defenseless. I felt like I'd done something awful like drowning a kitten. Matt's like that—like some little kitten. Or like Bambi. It's like hurting him would be the worst thing in the world.

So I cleaned him up, and found the least dirty shirt in the laundry basket for him to put on. And because I felt so bad, I was really rough with him, and I couldn't get him to stop crying. He was still crying when I walked him to school. And of course we were late—I've got detention for the rest of the week for being tardy. That means I'm not going to be able to pick Matt up after school today, tomorrow, or Friday. So I can't stop worrying. He *is* seven, of course, which should be old enough to walk home by himself—I was walking home by myself at seven—but, you know, somehow he doesn't even seem as old as I was at five.

I hope he's not still crying. The other kids make fun of him, I know they do. Maybe I'll stop at Sackbury's after detention tonight and buy him a bag of Snickers. They're his favorite. At least then he'll know I'm not mad at him anymore.

I tried to tell Sandy about all of this with Matt, and she looked at me weird and said, "Hey, he's just your brother, not your son. Can't you let your mom take care of him for once?" She's still kind of mad at me because I insisted we take Matt to the mall with us on Sunday, and I wouldn't let her shoplift with him around. And there was this great hot pink miniskirt she really, really wanted, but didn't have enough money for.

I don't know why she was so upset. It was no skin off her nose. She just went back and got the skirt on Monday.

Tish,

I appreciate the amount of writing you're doing in here. But do you think that every once in a while you might write an entry that you would allow me to read? I don't expect you to reveal anything you don't want to reveal, but I would like to know how this journal-keeping is going for you.

SEPTEMBER 22

Yes, Mrs. Dunphrey, you CAN read this entry.

Well, it's hard to believe that school has been going on for almost an entire month now. I feel like I've learned so much. Ha, ha.

You wanted to know how this journal-keeping is going for me—okay, I guess. I know everyone's complaining about having to do two entries a week. But hey, you're the teacher, right? You could make us do five a week if you wanted, right? (That ISN'T a suggestion.)

I'm sorry, I really don't have much else to say. I'll write more later.

SEPTEMBER 23

Don't read this, Mrs. Dunphrey.

Geez, was yesterday's entry bogus or what? You shouldn't take it personal or anything. For a teacher, you're not too bad. I mean, you don't yell at us like Mrs. Rachethead does, and you at least try to make things interesting. It's not your fault that none of us really care about Shakespeare or—who's that other guy you were talking about today? Faulkner? Neither one of them has anything to do with my life, as far as I can tell. Did either of them have a father that left them and a mother that might as well be a zombie? Did either of them have to work at a dumb job like mine, frying up thousands and thousands of French fries for all the kids who don't have to work? I don't think so.

But anyhow, because you're a teacher and all, I'm not going to write anything for you to see that really says anything. For all I know, you could go tell someone Mom's mistreating Matt and me, just because she's not there to fix us breakfast every morning. Something like that happened to Rachel Samson—she went and told Mrs. Rhodes that her father beat her when she got a D in math, and Mrs. Rhodes reported it to some state agency. Next thing you know, there was some social worker nosing around, asking all Rachel's friends if Mr. Samson molested her. Rachel was so embarrassed, she didn't come to school for a week.

So—I know you're not reading this, but if you were, I'd have to say that you shouldn't feel bad that I'm not letting you read what I really think about.

SEPTEMBER 25

Don't read this, Mrs. Dunphrey.

I can't believe this happened. I still feel sick. Bud Turner asked me out.

Bud Turner, who I know I've never mentioned here before because he is so gross that I don't even want to think about him—Bud Turner is my boss at the Burger Boy. I mean, he's old enough to be my father, but he still has more pimples than Robbie Richards (the guy everyone calls Clearasil Face behind his back). And he's not that tall, but he must weigh 200 pounds—you can tell he's eaten way too many Burger Boys and Big Burger Boys in his lifetime.

Bud is just the assistant manager, not the manager, but he acts like he's totally in charge. Last night it was just him and me working, because he sent Charmaine Stewart home when things got really slow. I was cleaning out the shake machine, and Bud came up behind me.

"Tish," he says in kind of a sappy voice. I thought he was just going to tell me something else to do, like mop the floor or wait on a customer—he's big on telling everyone else to do something when he doesn't do anything himself. So I stopped working and looked him right in the face.

"Tish, you're really pretty," he says. "Wanna go see a movie with me sometime?"

"I don't go to movies," I said. Which was a lie, but who cares? I turned around and pretended to be scrubbing real hard on the inside of the shake machine.

"It doesn't have to be a movie," he said. "I'd just like to go out with you."

And I said, "No way, José. Not in a million years."

He got mad, of course, and started asking why I had to be so mean about it. It was kind of funny, actually. He was almost begging, like Matt does when I tell him to go to bed and he wants to stay up and watch another hour of TV.

I told my friends about it, and Rochelle told me I should file a sexual harassment suit against Bud. Is it sexual harassment if your boss asks you out? Sandy laughed and said I was being stupid—she said I should have gone out with him. Then maybe I could get off work whenever I want, and maybe he'd make Charmaine clean out the bathroom all the time instead of me always doing it. Sandy said, "You should take advantage of the advantages you have."

Except, I'd rather clean out the bathrooms a million times than go out with Bud Turner even once.

SEPTEMBER 28

Don't read this, Mrs. Dunphrey.

I am so pissed. The work schedule for the next two weeks was posted today, and guess who got her hours cut back to five a week? Uh-huh—me. And guess whose job it is to make up the work schedule? That's right—Bud Turner's.

I was so mad when I saw the schedule posted above our punch cards, I was shaking. The only thing that stopped me from storming into Bud's office and calling him every name in the book—and then quitting—was that I'm saving up to buy Matt a Nintendo for his birthday next month. Maybe I should have cussed Bud out, anyhow—working five hours a week, I'll never have enough for even the cheapest Nintendo. I called Rochelle and said, "How do you file a sexual harassment suit?" Then Mr. Seagrave, the manager, came out of his office and told me with so many customers waiting, I wasn't allowed to make a personal call. Maybe I should have picked a better time, but I said I needed to talk to him urgently.

I've always liked Mr. Seagrave—I don't know why he

ever hired Bud—but he wasn't very sympathetic. He gave me a whole song and dance about how everybody's hours are being cut back a little, because business has been slower lately—"and if we don't sell burgers, we don't make enough money to pay our employees." Yeah, right. In an hour, I make the equivalent of exactly one Big Burger Boy with a side order of fries (and that's a small side order, too). I pointed out that Charmaine was still getting eighteen hours a week, and so were four or five other people.

"If you don't like the way things are run around here, you don't have to work here," Mr. Seagrave said.

That was really low. I was all ready to say, "Okay, I quit." It would have been so much fun to just turn around, yank off my apron, and leave. But then I thought, "Nintendo. Matt." I straightened up, looked Mr. Seagrave right in the eye, and said in my best sweet-talk voice, "I understand that, Mr. Seagrave. Would you mind speaking to Bud anyway?"

And then I did turn around and leave. I was very dignified.

OCTOBER 1

Don't read this, Mrs. Dunphrey.

Surprise, surprise. Bud posted a revised work schedule today and strangely enough, my hours were raised to fifteen a week. It's still not that great, but it's certainly better than five. I felt like doing a victory dance, or something. But then Bud sent me out into the dining room to clean up a table where the whole football team from Gable had been eating—talk about a mess! They'd mixed gobs of ketchup and mustard and used it to fingerpaint on the chairs. And then they'd unscrewed the lids on the salt and pepper shakers and poured barbecue sauce in the shakers and on about fifty napkins . . . It took me an hour to clean up. Even so, I still felt good. I told Rochelle about getting more hours, and now she's calling me a "warrior for womankind." Who would have guessed Rochelle—Rochelle, who spends two hours a day, I swear, putting on make-up and curling her hair—who would have guessed she was such a feminist?

I am feeling so very, very good tonight. I brought home a sackful of Burger Boys and fries for Matt and me, and we sat around telling knock-knock jokes. For some reason he thinks every single one is just hilarious, even if it's just something stupid I made up. He laughed hardest at, "Knock, knock—who's there?—Burger—Burger who?—Burger Boy." I don't even know why it was funny, but he was laughing so much I had to laugh, too.

And then Mom looked over from where she was watching TV, and she said, "Knock-knock."

"Who's there?" Matt said.

"No one," Mom said.

That kind of scared me, because Mom had such a weird look in her eye. But Matt screamed out, "No one who?"

"No one's as funny as you two," Mom said.

And then we all laughed, and it seemed like maybe for

once, for the first time in years, everything might be all right in the Bonner house.

Oops—I just realized—I wrote five entries this time. Oh well. Bonus for you. I'll have to watch it—I don't want you thinking I like this journal stuff.

Tish,

Fine. Glad you're writing so much.

OCTOBER 6

Please don't read this, Mrs. Dunphrey.

I can't believe I thought things were going to be all right. I came home from school today and Mom was sitting in the rocking chair in the living room, not even watching TV, just rocking back and forth, back and forth. I asked her if she was okay, and she said, "He's back in town."

Of course I knew she meant my dad. "So?" I said. "Who cares?"

That made Mom mad. "Who cares? Who cares? I do. You should—he's your father, for God's sake."

I told Matt to go to his room and do his homework. Matt got all whiny—"I don't want to . . . Can't I go see my daddy?" Matt's so young, he doesn't even remember what having Dad around was like. He just has this idea it's like on TV—those *Cosby Show* reruns maybe—where the father's all nice and kind and helpful. Matt should know our mom's not like TV mothers—why should Dad be like TV dads? In the end, I got Matt to leave.

"So what are you going to do?" I asked Mom. I put it just the way I'd put it with Rochelle or Chastity or Sandy, when they're worrying about their boyfriends.

"I don't know . . . What should I do?" Mom said. Same old wimpy Mom as ever. "I've got to see him. Maybe he'll move back in . . ."

I just snorted and went to my room. I wished Granma was still alive. She could tell Mom how dumb she was being about Dad. Of course, Mom didn't listen to her, either.

OCTOBER 7

Don't read this, Mrs. Dunphrey.

It's all Mom's fault—I can't stop thinking about Dad. I've been trying to remember a time when he wasn't mean, when he and Mom weren't fighting, when he wasn't always yelling at someone. And I kind of can. When I was little—real little, maybe two or three—Dad had a job driving a cement truck. I called it a round-and-round truck, and Dad used to laugh about that. In a good way. Like he was proud of me. I remember one time, he took me and Mom for a ride in his round-and-round truck, and we all sat in the cab eating Cheetos. If I close my eyes, I can almost see us, all laughing, getting the orangy Cheetos dust all over our hands and faces, nobody caring. I was happy. I think Mom and Dad were, too.

So what happened after that? Any other time I ever remember, if I'd been eating Cheetos and getting messy, Dad would have been yelling about what a slob I was and how Mom just didn't know how to take care of me. Why'd he have to change?

I do know he got fired from driving the round-and-round truck. It was after that we all came to live with Granma.

OCTOBER 12

Don't read this, Mrs. Dunphrey.

Mom's going to do something stupid, I know she is.

She's missed work the last three nights—I had to call in

sick for her, because she forgot to do that. She just sits in the rocking chair rocking, muttering things like, "I could see him . . . It could work . . ." It really wasn't a lie for me to tell her boss that she was sick, because she hasn't been sleeping or eating, and she looks really terrible. I was trying to be funny, and I told her, "Mom, if you do go see Dad, do yourself a favor. Take a shower and put on some makeup first."

I shouldn't have said that, because then she started sobbing, and went running to the bathroom. She locked the door, and I know she was staring in the mirror because she kept screaming, "I'm too ugly for him now . . ." Then she had the shower on for almost forty-five minutes. I was half afraid she'd try to slit her wrists or something. The only good thing is, I don't think Mom would ever have the nerve for that.

I've been trying to keep Matt away from Mom while she's acting so scary. Last night I didn't have to work, and I kept Matt at the mall until it closed. He got all whiny—"Ti-ish, can't we go home? My feet hurt." But at least when we did get home, he went to bed and fell asleep right away, and didn't hear Mom at all.

I tried to ask Chastity and Rochelle and Sandy what they would do if they had my problem, without letting them know how freaked out Mom really is. "Do your mothers ever act weird?" I asked them.

Sandy just kind of snorted and said, "Mothers are made to be weird." And then Chastity started telling this long story about how her mother doesn't like Chastity to use so much hairspray or pouf her bangs up so high, because she thinks it's slutty. That's why Chastity waits until she gets to school to do her hair right.

"No. I mean really weird," I said. But it was lost on them. What'd I expect? All they really care about is makeup and boys. They're no smarter than me. How were they going to have any great answers?

OCTOBER 15

I wish so bad that Granma were still alive. She would know what to do about Mom. Granma used to take care of all of us so well. I remember for a long time after we first moved in with Granma, I was scared of the dark. And Granma would come in every night and say, "What do you think is in the dark that's so scary?" And I'd say goblins, or bogeymen, and she'd wave her arms and say, "They're gone. All gone." And the way she said it, I believed her. I'd smell her old-lady perfume—lavender or lilac, something like that—when she waved her arms, and it seemed like the scent would protect me from any bad thing. And after a while, I ran out of bad things to be scared of.

Now that I think of it, I don't think Dad was living with us when we first moved in with Granma. That was later.

Tish,

I'm delighted that you finally let me read a "real" entry in this journal. I've felt frustrated seeing almost all your previous entries marked "don't read," because I can tell you're writing a lot. But of course I've wanted to respect your wish for privacy.

Based on this one entry, I think you may have a knack for writing—a knack you've managed to hide in practically everything else you've handed in. Perhaps you've needed the power of a childhood memory to stir you. Whatever, I think you ought to consider trying out for the literary magazine staff here—probably you've seen it, The Lodestar*? You could make quite a contribution. Talk to me if you're interested.*

You're rather vague here about the problem with your mother (and father?). I don't want to pry, but you know there are lots of people here at the school who are ready and willing to help you with any personal problem(s). You could go to one of the counselors or take advantage of the new Student Assistance Program. Or if you'd feel more comfortable talking to someone your own age, the peer counselors might help. And of course, I'd be perfectly willing to talk to you, if you want. Just don't assume you have to handle everything by yourself.

OCTOBER 21

Do NOT read this, Mrs. Dunphrey.

I can't believe I forgot to put the "don't read this" label on my last entry. How dumb can I be? So now Mrs. Dunphrey knows I'm having problems. Great. She kept looking at me funny all during class today, and I didn't know why until she handed the journals back and I saw what I'd done. Hey, Mrs. Dunphrey, everyone has problems, okay? Leave me alone.

I'm so embarrassed that she made all those suggestions for where I could go for help. The counselors? Yeah, right Like Mrs. Herzenberger has time for anyone. Last year when I went in to show her what classes I wanted for this year, the whole conversation was, "Um-hm, um-hm. Okay. Fine. Can you send the next student in?" Or, wait—I'm supposed to go to the peer counselors? That's the biggest joke of all. Everybody knows the peer counselors are the worst gossips in the whole school. Just look at poor Ronda Hartshorn. She talked to Heather Owens and Mitch Ramirez "strictly confidentially" and, funny, next thing Ronda knew, everybody in the school had heard she was pregnant and thinking about having an abortion. Poor Ronda. Even Mr. Tremont tried to give her advice.

So, thanks but no thanks, Mrs. Dunphrey. I can handle my problems all by myself. I may not do a great job, but they stay my problems.

At least I didn't say too much in that last entry. It's just about Granma and the bogeymen and the smell of her perfume. I guess there are a lot more embarrassing entries I could have let Mrs. Dunphrey read by mistake.

Isn't it hilarious that she thinks I should try out for *The Lodestar?* Like Megan Satterthwaite, with her $150 sweaters, would let me within 100 feet of that thing. Like I'd want to hang out with those snobs. Like I even care about writing anything.

OCTOBER 23

Don't read this, Mrs. Dunphrey.

Can't you give it a rest? When you asked me to stay after class today, I was sure I was in trouble. But no, you just wanted to talk about *The Lodestar* again. And how I should be on the honor roll, not barely passing. Right.

The funniest thing was when you asked if it'd help to talk to my parents. How'd you put it—"I know most teenagers are hesitant to acknowledge their parents, but sometimes parental involvement is necessary. Sometimes parents and teachers need to work as a team . . ." Sometimes, Mrs. Dunphrey, you talk like a book. I can just see you and my mom getting together. It makes me crack up. Let's see, here's Mrs. Dunphrey with her silky blouses and classy skirts and big words. And here's my mom in her ragged jeans and her "ain'ts" and "she don'ts." You'd say "academic potential" and my mom's eyes would just go blank. She'd say, "Huh?" about fifty times.

Or let's say you got real ambitious and hunted down my

dad. Supposing you found him, you'd be real impressed with his beer company cap and his old ripped flannel shirts and long johns. (That's about the fanciest clothes I ever remember seeing him wear.) He'd say, "Tish who?"

Come on, Mrs. Dunphrey. Give up.

Today is Matt's birthday. I picked him up after school and then we took the bus to McDonald's. (He likes that better than Burger Boy, even though I can't get an employee discount at McDonald's—I guess Matt gets sick of Burger Boy burgers because I bring them home all the time.) I told him he could get whatever he wanted, so he ordered a Big Mac and a large fries and a big strawberry milk shake. He didn't finish any of it. But, hey, it's his birthday. I told him nothing mattered today. I wouldn't yell at him over anything.

"You don't yell at me, Tish," he said.

"Yes, I do," I said. "You don't have to be nice. I know I yell at you a lot more than I should."

"But only because you want me to be good," he said. And he smiled in this way he has, where he shows his side teeth, and he looked so little and cute and innocent. I think he got that idea about being yelled at for his own good at school. Anyway, it made me feel like I'm not so bad to him after all.

I couldn't get him the Nintendo, because I couldn't save enough money in time. (Maybe I would have been able to, if Mom would give Matt and me lunch money, instead of me always paying for everything.) Instead, I got him a baseball mitt. I thought it was kind of a stupid present—I just couldn't think of anything else. But Matt got all excited. He said all the other boys at school have mitts, but he didn't think he'd ever get one. He fell asleep hugging it.

Maybe I'll be able to afford a Nintendo for Matt for Christmas.

OCTOBER 24

Don't you dare read this, Mrs. Dunphrey.

Well, Mom's gone and done it. While I had Matt at McDonald's last night, she started driving around town looking for Dad. She found him down at the Alibi Inn on Sidell Street—it's a horrid bar, all smoky and gross. I'm sure you wouldn't know anything about it, Mrs. Dunphrey. I don't know what Mom told Dad—I don't want to know—but this morning when I got up and walked into the kitchen, he was sitting at the kitchen table eating eggs and toast, sort of normal, like he'd never been away at all.

I just stopped and stared at him.

"Is that how you greet your dad, when you haven't seen him in two years?" Dad asked, all sweet and nice.

Hey, it's not my fault I hadn't seen him in two years. "Hi, Dad," I said. Cautious.

I didn't know it, but Matt was right behind me. And as soon as I said that, Matt came out in front of me, "Dad? Daddy?"

Then he ran over to Dad and gave him one of those big

hugs only a kid can give. Totally trusting. Dad swung him up on his lap and said, "Now, that's more like it."

"It's really you?" Matt said. Dad nodded and let Matt hug him again. I could have cried right then and there, the way Matt was acting. He looked happier than I'd seen him in years. I guess I'd stopped noticing how sad his eyes looked all the time. Matt grinned and grinned and grinned. I wanted to grab him away and scream, "No—don't. You can't trust him." Then Mom came in from taking the trash out, and she was grinning too, like a big fool. Am I the only one in the whole family who remembers anything?

"So where have you been?" I asked. "It has been a while."

I was waiting for him to yell at me for my smart mouth—the sarcasm was dripping—but Dad just shrugged.

"I got a job driving coast to coast," he said. "Oranges from Florida, pork bellies from Chicago—you name it."

And then he started telling us stories about his adventures, how he'd outsmarted a robber in Flagstaff, Arizona, and how he'd gotten trapped in a blizzard out in Burlington, Vermont. And it was like no one but me thought it was weird that he was back now, that he'd never even sent a postcard the whole time he was away. Matt kept beaming, holding on to Dad's leg, and Mom sat beside them, reaching out every now and then to touch Dad's hair. Like she couldn't believe he was real.

I stayed back by the door. I think I was thinking I could get away fast if I needed to. Except I'd want to take Matt with me.

OCTOBER 27

Don't read this, Mrs. Dunphrey.

While I was working at the Burger Boy last night, Dad took Matt over to Children's Palace and bought him a big Nintendo system, even better than the one I was going to get. When I got home from work, Dad had it all set up, and they were playing some video game that had to do with saving the world from invading aliens.

Matt wanted me to come play with them, but I told him it was past his bedtime.

"Any adult should know that," I said. And then I was scared, because that was the kind of thing that would have really set Dad off in the past. I was lucky—I don't think Dad heard me because the video game was so loud.

"Ti-ish, please play with us," Matt said.

"If she doesn't want to play, that's her problem," Dad said. "It's just more time for us, right? More father-son time. This is a boy's game—we don't need any girls."

"Right," Matt echoed. "No gi-irls allowed, Tish."

I went back to my bedroom so mad I wanted to hit somebody. I pounded on the bed over and over again, until Mom yelled, "Tish, stop that!"

And I couldn't yell back at her, either, because she and Dad are so lovey-dovey now he'd probably beat me if I said anything to her.

I wish I could be like Mom and Matt and just smile, smile, smile—who cares that Dad was gone for two years? He's back now. Who cares that he yelled all the time and broke dishes and hit Mom and sometimes even me? He's not hitting anybody now.

Yet.

If Granma were here, she'd be on my side. She'd tell Mom and Matt how stupid they're being.

Tish,

Okay. Do think about The Lodestar . . .

NOVEMBER 3

Don't read this, Mrs. Dunphrey.

Dad is still being really nice. He bought Matt a pirate costume and took him out trick-or-treating Saturday night. I went to a Halloween party with Rochelle and Chastity, and no one noticed that I didn't get home until 3 a.m.

Could real life be like this always? I can't believe in it.

I have noticed that Dad doesn't seem to have a job anymore. I don't know where he's getting the money to buy all those things for Matt. He bought me some perfume the other day, too, but I told him it wasn't a kind I use. It was White Sands—something for women a lot older than me.

NOVEMBER 6

Please don't read this, Mrs. Dunphrey.

I knew it was too good to last. Mom and Dad had a big fight last night. I came home from the Burger Boy, and Dad was throwing things at Mom—his shoes, one of the lamps, a decorative Elvis plate Mom had to go and order off the TV.

"Where's Matt?" I asked right away. Dad yelled at me—something about how I was probably worse than my mother. I thought he was going to throw one of Granma's old flowerpots at me. I ran to my room and slammed the door. Then, when I was sure Dad hadn't followed me, I crept down to Matt's room. Matt was in there, hiding under the bed crying.

I pulled him out and made him sit on the bed with me. He had lint in his hair, and his eyes were all swollen and red, like he'd been crying for hours. I wanted to march back out to the living room and tell Mom and Dad to shut up, or leave, or something—anything to quit scaring Matt. Instead I held my hands over his ears.

"That's not Daddy out there," Matt told me.

"Oh yeah?" I said.

"No, it's a bad man. Daddy gives me presents."

What was I supposed to say to that? After a while, Matt said, "What are they fighting about?"

I'd been trying not to listen, but I would have had to have been deaf not to hear some of it. Mom was all whimpers now—pitiful apologies—but Dad was going on and on in a loud voice about Haggarty's and someone Mom worked with. I think Dad thought Mom two-timed him while he was away. That's so crazy. I don't think she's looked at another man, ever, maybe—but so what if she did? He was away for two years! What'd he expect?

Anyhow, I told Matt they were fighting about grown-up stuff. I told him he'd have to be a lot older to understand.

"Do you understand?" he asked. "You're a lot older than me."

The way he looked at me with his innocent eyes, I could have cried. I don't want him thinking that's how people are supposed to act. But what was I going to say—"Mom and Dad are horrible people"? They are horrible. I hate them—hate them, hate them, hate them! I wish they would both run away to Flagstaff, Arizona, or Burlington, Vermont. Maybe I even wish they were dead. I don't care where they go, how bad they ruin their own lives. But do they have to ruin everything for Matt and me, too?

NOVEMBER 9

Don't you dare read this, Mrs. Dunphrey.

Well, it looks like it's Monday night at the fights. Again. Tonight, Dad didn't like the way Mom cooked his spaghetti. Last night, she didn't turn the TV on right away when he asked her to. The night before—I don't even remember what the fight was about the night before. Except, every night, Matt and I hide in his room. At first, I tried to read to him, play games with him, anything to keep him from hearing them in the living room. But he just stares at the Dr. Seuss pages, he forgets to take his turn in Candyland. I have trouble remembering, too.

Tonight Matt asked me, "How much more do they have to fight about?"

It's like he thinks there's some end I can tell him about, like medicine you only have to take for two weeks. Even if it tastes awful, you can choke it down thinking, "Only ten more times, only nine more times, only . . ."

I told Matt I didn't know how they could possibly have anything left to fight about. But that's not true. The more I listen to them fight, the madder I feel. I don't think I could ever get rid of that mad, even if I went out and screamed at them for the rest of my life. I've started thinking crazy things. Tony Brill next door has a whole gun collection. I could just borrow one of them. I wouldn't even have to shoot anyone, just use it to scare Mom and Dad, just make them shut up. I lie in bed at night and I picture me holding them hostage, at gunpoint. I'd tie them up and gag their mouths so they wouldn't be able to yell. Or—better yet—I'd let them talk to one another, but only in good ways. I'd say, "Talk nice." Granma used to say that to Matt and me.

I scare myself. I think if I had a gun, I really might use it.

Maybe I'm not any better than Dad or Mom.

NOVEMBER 12

Don't read this, Mrs. Dunphrey.

Last night I remembered why Granma taught me to crochet.

She was always crocheting something—both Matt and me have baby blankets she made. Mine is pink with white bows and his is green with fruit shapes on it. And every year at Christmas and for our birthdays, we'd get something else crocheted—mittens, scarves, sweaters. I was proud of them, until about third grade when one of the other girls, Heather Richards, I think it was, made fun of me having everything homemade. I started hinting to Granma that I'd rather have something store-bought. It'd be easier, I said. Why did she have to crochet all the time?

"It's better than hitting someone," she told me.

That was a time kind of like now, when Mom and Dad were fighting about everything. It didn't seem so bad then, because Granma was always there, telling Matt and me stories, singing songs to us so we didn't hear Mom and Dad. (She didn't forget to turn the Dr. Seuss pages.)

But then one day, Dad came home and Mom was out somewhere, at the grocery maybe, and he started yelling at me. And I yelled back. I told him to shut up. I told him he was bad. And then he hit me so hard it knocked me across the kitchen. I still have a little scar on my forehead where I hit the table.

Granma was there right away, and she took me away and washed the blood off my face. Then that night she gave me a crochet hook and some orange yarn and said, "Here, let me show you how to do a chain stitch . . ." She said more, she said, "You can control the yarn, even if you can't control anything else."

And then for a long time, both of us crocheted every night, back in Granma's room. Matt would hide in the yarn between us. He said it was better than listening to songs or books. He said in the yarn, he couldn't hear anything.

It all sounds so stupid now. Did Granma really think I could solve anything by crocheting?

Did she ever solve anything?

Tish,

Okay. I would appreciate getting to read another of your entries sometime soon. I know I said you could mark every entry "Don't read," if you wanted—but do you really have to?

NOVEMBER 18

DON'T read this, Mrs. Dunphrey.

So you'd appreciate the chance to get to read one of my entries, Mrs. Dunphrey? Oh great, wonderful. I'm sure they'd make you very happy. Oh, isn't this precious, you could say, how well Tish writes about her parents' fights. "Tish," you'd ask, "would you mind if *The Lodestar* reprinted that wonderful description of you and your brother cowering in his room while your father throws flowerpots at your mother? It's so exquisitely done." Or wait, maybe if you read my journal, you'd understand why I'm not exactly keeping up with Julius Caesar right now. What would you do then—say, "Sure, Tish, you don't have to read Act II. I understand completely"? Would you stop calling on me? Would you stop looking disappointed when I don't know the difference between Cassius or Brutus or anyone else?

Mrs. Dunphrey, I don't really dislike you. It's just, your problem is you're too innocent. You're even worse than Matt. You look out at us in the classroom and you think we're all there ready and eager to learn about literature and grammar. I don't know, maybe we would be, if we weren't too busy thinking about our real lives. It's not just me, either. I'm not the only one whose parents fight all the time. There are other kids who can't think about Julius Caesar because they're worrying about their parents being out of work. Or they're afraid they're pregnant. Or they're on drugs.

Hey, we're all just your basic wonderful kids, with your

basic wonderful lives. If you think anyone's being honest in the journal entries they let you see, you're really fooling yourself. I'm probably the only one writing anything real at all in here. And I'm not really sure why I do. I guess it's like my Granma said about crocheting. It is better than hitting someone.

And if I thought for a minute that anyone would read this, I'd destroy it so fast your head would spin.

But, okay, if it really makes you happy, I'll give you one entry, Mrs. Dunphrey. It's going to be the fakest entry anybody ever wrote.

NOVEMBER 19

Yes, you MAY read this, Mrs. Dunphrey.

Today I'm going to write about Thanksgiving. Thanksgiving is just a week away. It's wonderful because we get out of school for two days. Hurrah! (No offense, Mrs. Dunphrey. I'm sure we'll all miss your class.) And everybody gets to eat like pigs. At my house, we'll get up early and watch the parades on TV. I like the one from New York, the Macy's parade, but my mom always likes to watch the one in Hawaii. She wants to go to Hawaii someday.

The whole time we're watching the parades, the house fills up with really great smells, of turkey roasting and pumpkin pies baking, and sweet potatoes cooking . . . I'm making myself hungry just thinking about it. When it finally is time to eat, we all go around the table saying what we're thankful for this year. Then we dig in and eat, and don't get up until we are full to bursting.

NOVEMBER 23

Don't read this entry, Mrs. Dunphrey.

I showed Rochelle the last entry I wrote, the fake one, and she thought it was really sweet. (Oh, gag.) She asked me if we really did go around the table, saying what we're thankful for this year. She thought that was cute. Then I told her I'd made the whole thing up—I think I got the saying-what-we're-thankful-for bit from one of those Thanksgiving or Christmas TV specials. *The Waltons*, maybe.

Except, now that I think about it, it seems like Granma used to make us do that sometimes.

Tonight I took Matt with me when I went in to work at the Burger Boy. I told him to sit still and color or play with his Matchbox cars while he waited on me. He was really good and quiet—he didn't disturb anyone, not like a lot of the kids his age who come in with their parents. And I bought him a Coke and a burger, so it wasn't like he wasn't a paying customer. But Bud was still upset. He said my job while I'm at the Burger Boy is cashier, not babysitter, and if my first priority is taking care of my brother, then I shouldn't try to work at Burger Boy, too.

I don't think Bud's forgiven me yet for not going out with him. Maybe Sandy was right—maybe I should have gone out with him, so he would be nicer to me. And then I could take Matt to work with me every night.

Except, the funny thing is, it turned out Matt would have been fine staying at home tonight. When we got home Mom was just sitting in her chair in the living room watching TV, like always. She said Dad was out bowling. He hadn't even been home for supper. (Matt asked. I sure didn't care.)

NOVEMBER 26

Don't read this entry, Mrs. Dunphrey.

It's Thanksgiving—oh boy, what a great holiday at the Bonners'. Dad didn't come home again last night, and I don't know that Mom even bothered to go to sleep. When I went to bed, she was sitting and rocking in the living room, kind of in a trance, and when I got up this morning she was just the same. About 11:30 this morning I asked her if she was going to fix anything for Thanksgiving, and she looked at me like she didn't even know what I was talking about. So I went and got some stuff at Haggarty's—I was lucky, because they were going to close at noon. It was just deli turkey and instant potatoes and canned cranberry sauce and a store-bought pie, but it cost everything I had left from my last Burger Boy check. I just meant it to be for Matt and me, but when I was putting it on the table, Mom came out and ate with us.

And then an hour or so later, after Matt and I did all the dishes and put everything away, we heard Dad's pick-up outside. Mom had been acting like walking to the kitchen was about as much as we could expect out of her—she didn't even put her dirty plate in the sink. But as soon as Dad pulled up out front, she started scurrying around straightening up pictures on the wall, shoving these ratty old cushions of Granma's under the sofa, hiding the pile of *Soap Opera Digest*s under a chair. And she kept telling Matt and me, "Don't do anything to make your dad mad. He's got to see how much we love him. Then everything will be all right . . ."

I was all ready to say, "Sure, Mom. What if I don't love him?" But then Dad walked in, and Mom couldn't do anything but smile at him. He brought a big roast turkey and something like a vat of mashed potatoes and lots of other stuff: green beans, sweet potatoes, cranberry sauce, and three kinds of pie. I think he got it at some restaurant. It was a thousand times better than what I bought. And he was all jolly and friendly, like he thought he was Santa Claus. Matt started to say we'd already eaten, but Mom real fast clamped her hand over his mouth. She said things like, "Oh, what a wonderful surprise! Ray, you are the best husband and father any family could have!"

Yeah, right.

We all sat down and pretended to eat like we were really hungry. Matt kept looking at me like he was confused, but I kicked him under the table and shook my head. He got sick afterward and threw up all over the kitchen floor. My stomach didn't feel so hot, either.

Tish,

Okay. Fine.

DECEMBER 3

Don't read this, Mrs. Dunphrey.

Geez, I put all that effort into that one entry, and all I get is, "Okay. Fine"? Teachers are so weird.

Dad's still in his nice mode. That Thanksgiving dinner was just the beginning. He hasn't yelled at Mom in a week, or thrown anything. And Saturday he took Mom and Matt and me downtown to see the Christmas lights turned on for the first time. Then he took us out to eat—not fast food, but at a real sit-down place, Shoney's.

I don't trust him, though. He knows it, too. Sometimes he'll catch me looking at him—looking hard, because I'm trying to see how long this is going to last—and he says, "What? What? Didn't anyone teach you not to stare?" I think I make him nervous. Fine. He makes me nervous, too.

DECEMBER 5

Don't read this, Mrs. Dunphrey.

It's really late—2 a.m.–but I can't get to sleep. Sandy and I went to a party tonight at Eric Seaver's. Eric's parents are out of town for the weekend (fools!), so as you can imagine things got a little wild. It was fun—it should have been fun—but I don't know, I just felt sad all night long. I was there laughing and joking with everyone else, but it's like there was some part of me standing back, watching, thinking, "Is this as good as it gets?" Randy Seaver, Eric's older brother, was there, home from college—he goes to some school that lets out from

Thanksgiving until after New Year's—and he was kind of hitting on Sandy. Sandy has a boyfriend right now but Tony wasn't there (he was at some family thing), so Sandy was flirting like crazy with Randy. She kept saying things like, "Isn't it cute how our names rhyme? Randy and Sandy—Mmm!" At midnight he kissed her—he said he got confused and thought it was New Year's Eve—and someone actually started singing that song from grade school, "Randy and Sandy, sitting in a tree, K, I, S, S, I, N, G . . ."

Pretty soon after that, I told Sandy I wanted to go home, and she got mad and said I was jealous because Randy liked her, not me. I told her that was crazy—Randy's not even that cute. He has weird hair that sticks up straight, and he talks like he thinks everyone but him is dumb. Anyhow, I had to get Merry Rogers to take me home, because Sandy stayed with Randy. Tony's going to kill her on Monday when he hears how she was acting.

But you know what? I think I *was* kind of jealous of Sandy. It's not that I wanted Randy Seaver. (Oh—he sniffs all the time, too, because he's got some sort of allergies. Five minutes with him makes you want to yell, "Use a Kleenex!") And it's not that I really think he's that madly in love with Sandy. But it'd be nice to have someone who cared about me, someone I could talk to about anything, someone who'd tell me I was really special. Rochelle reads those dippy romance novels all the time, and sometimes she loans one to me. I pretend I think they're stupid, but they make me cry, because the guys in those stories really do love their women. They'd do anything for them. In one story Rochelle gave me last year, the hero rode fifty miles in a blizzard because the heroine was trapped in an avalanche. And he found her and saved her and they made love, right there in the snow . . . Except, I really do know that kind of thing is stupid. How many romances in real life are any good? You'd have to say Mom is about as devoted to Dad as anyone can be, and what's it get her? Bruises, is all I see.

DECEMBER 8

Don't read this, Mrs. Dunphrey.

I'm going to do Christmas shopping tonight after school. I'm probably going to get perfume or earrings for Sandy and Rochelle and Chastity, and a robe for Mom, and a Gameboy for Matt, since he already has a Nintendo now.

I'm not getting anything for Dad.

He wasn't home last night or the night before, but I couldn't get up the nerve to ask Mom where he was. She had to work double shifts at Haggarty's, because I guess some of the other cashiers are sick. So yesterday and last night, it was like it was just Matt and me living together. I didn't have to work at the Burger Boy, even. Last night we sat at the kitchen table and did homework together. Anyone who knows me would have laughed—Tish Bonner, actually doing homework?—but it was kind of cozy, him working on addition, me working on geometry. Matt finished first (eight-year-olds never have much homework) and then he sat there drawing while he waited on me to get done. Matt's in LD classes, and sometimes I'm afraid he really is dumb, but he can draw better than anyone I know. (Maybe I should get him some sort of art set, instead of a Gameboy. I'll have to think about that.) I made cocoa, and we put, like, ten thousand marshmallows in it, and there was no one to yell at us.

All that reminds me how, when I was about Matt's age and Matt was a cute little baby, I used to dream about Mom and Dad leaving and it being just Matt and me and Granma. I used to think that if I did everything right—didn't step on any cracks walking home from school, remembered to put the forks the right way when I set the table, didn't talk back when Dad spanked me—if I did all those things, maybe I'd wake up some morning and it'd be like Mom and Dad never existed, and we were just Granma's kids.

Except, Granma would have yelled at us about eating too many marshmallows.

DECEMBER 10

Don't read this, Mrs. Dunphrey.

Still haven't seen Dad all week. Mom's stayed in bed the last few days. She says she's sick—says she got the flu everyone else had. But I don't know. I hear her crying in there. It scares Matt.

Tony broke up with Sandy when he heard how she'd been all over Randy Seaver at the party Saturday night. And then Sandy called Randy Seaver and he was like, "Who?" Like he'd never heard of her in his life. (Of course, Sandy didn't admit that—Rochelle told me, because Rochelle was right there when

Sandy called him.) Sandy went to the mall and shoplifted a necklace and a pair of $35 earrings, to make herself feel better. She was real obvious about it, too. It's a wonder she didn't get caught.

I knew real-life romances never worked out.

I remember the stories Granma used to tell about her and Granpa. He was in the Navy, and he had to be away sometimes for six or eight months at a time. But he wrote her every single day while he was on board ship. And even though he could have ended up being someone really important in the Navy—do they have generals?—he decided to quit that because he couldn't stand being away from Granma. When he got home, he worked two jobs for a while so they could save enough to buy a house. It's the house we live in right now.

I always liked hearing those stories from Granma, but now—this is kind of scary—now sometimes I think, what if she only told me the good parts? Granpa died when I was only a year or two old, so I never really knew him. What if most of the time he treated Granma the way Dad treats Mom?

I think I would have been able to tell, the way Granma talked about Granpa. I don't think Granma would have put up with what Mom puts up with.

Tish,

These are fine. I'm glad to see that you're writing so much. I hope this journal is serving as a release for you. I know life can sometimes seem very difficult when you're in high school. It's very healthy to write things out.

DECEMBER 16

DON'T read this, Mrs. Dunphrey.

That was an odd note Mrs. Dunphrey wrote after my last entries. You don't suppose she's been reading some of this, do you? (Geez, who am I asking about that? You'd think I thought this journal is a real person.) I asked Rochelle and Chastity how they were doing their journals—I knew better than to ask Sandy, because she's not doing one at all. Says it's such a small part of her grade it doesn't matter, and anyhow, she doesn't care if she flunks. But that's Sandy for you. Both Rochelle and Chastity said they just write any dumb thing that comes to their minds, and they don't bother writing "Don't read" at the top of their entries. Chastity said she wrote a whole entry, "I love Mike Hunter, I love Mike Hunter," maybe fifty times, and Mrs. Dunphrey didn't care.

If I was Chastity, I'd be way embarrassed about that.

But maybe I should be more careful, even with the "Don't read" label. I should be more careful, anyhow, since I carry this notebook around, and I guess anyone could end up taking it and reading it. Sabra Carson picked up my stack of notebooks and books instead of hers in the bathroom the other day—it was an honest mistake, since we both had our geometry book, our English book, and blue notebooks. Sabra's okay, and she didn't have my books for more than about five seconds. But what if she'd opened my notebook and seen something I wrote about Dad being away, or about him hitting Mom? I'd die if people knew.

I'm going to tape the old entries together. And then I'm only going to write dumb things, like Chastity and Rochelle do. It's not like it matters, anyhow.

DECEMBER 18

Don't read this, Mrs. Dunphrey.

Everybody's dying for Christmas vacation. I don't know why the stupid school board won't let us out until the day before Christmas Eve. There's a Christmas party tonight. Should be a great time. I'm not going with Sandy, though. Maybe I'll go with Chastity and Mike, except I'll feel like a third wheel.

I wish I had a car. I'll be sixteen next Wednesday. (Hurray!) But then I have to take driver's ed. And anyhow, who can afford their own car? (Besides Sandy, I mean.) Sandy told me if I'd only gone out with Bud Turner, he'd probably let me borrow his car—he's a jerk, all right, but he does drive a cool car. A Camaro. 1967. Bright red. It just doesn't look right with him at the wheel.

DECEMBER 21

Don't read, Mrs. Dunphrey.

Mrs. Dunphrey said in class today that we won't have to hand this in again until after Christmas—I guess teachers get lazy around holidays too, huh? (Just joking, in case you *are* reading this.) So I won't have to write at all over Christmas break, and then I'll only have to do one entry after we get back . . .

It's good I'm ahead on this, because I'm behind on everything else. We have finals the week after we get back from break, and I don't know if I'll be able to pass any of them, it's been so long since I've paid attention in any of my classes. It's not my fault, though. I have personal things going on. Things beyond my control.

DECEMBER 28

DON'T YOU DARE READ THIS, Mrs. Dunphrey.

I know I decided I wasn't going to write anything real in here anymore, and I know it's crazy to touch any school stuff over break. But things are so bad, I feel like I'm going to explode if I don't do something. And sometimes it did used to make me feel a little better if I wrote things down . . .

Dad's gone. For good this time, I think. And it's all my fault—at least, Mom thinks it's all my fault.

We didn't see him for two weeks, then he waltzed in on Christmas Eve with a bunch of presents and a live Christmas tree. I swear, he even dressed up like Santa Claus. He came in saying, "Ho, ho, ho—has everyone in this house been good this year?" And then he started handing out presents—fancy ones. You could tell he'd had the clerks at the mall wrap them for him.

Maybe if Matt had looked happy, I would have kept my big mouth shut. But he didn't. He looked confused. He reminded me of this puppy the Rockholds down the street used to have—Joey Rockhold hated having to take the dog for a walk, so he'd take it out on the dog, jerking his chain first one way, then the other. The dog would try to go the way Joey wanted him to go, but it was impossible. As soon as the dog started in one direction, Joey jerked him another way. That dog eventually got so mean, the Rockholds had to have him put to sleep. I always thought it was Joey's fault.

So, anyhow, that's how Matt looked, like that confused puppy. He didn't know if he was supposed to run up to Dad and play along with the Santa Claus stuff, or if he was supposed to hang back with me because Dad would only be here for a little while. It's like Dad had chains on all of us, and he was jerking us all around. Mom did run over to him and talk about how beautiful the presents were, and how he really shouldn't have, but even she looked a little baffled and scared. I decided no chains, no faking for me.

I went over to Dad and I actually kind of shoved his chest a little—I was mad, and stupid—and I said, "We don't need you. We were having a great Christmas Eve without you." (That wasn't really true. I'd tried to make Christmas cookies for Matt, but I didn't put enough flour in, or something, and they were all too runny or burnt. And the presents I bought looked measly under that stupid silver tree we still have from when I was little. Mom didn't get anybody anything, because she lost her Christmas money, and Matt just had some homemade stuff.) Then I said, "Who asked you to come here?"

Dad looked a little confused himself for a minute—he's not used to being stood up to. Or maybe I just couldn't tell what he was thinking behind the Santa beard. Then he said, "For your information, your mother asked me to come here. And last time I checked, we are the parents and we make the decisions around here."

"Funny thing," I said. "There must not need to be any decisions made except once a month or so."

And then he hit me, knocked me back into the tree. I landed on the box that had Mom's robe in it and smashed it. Matt screamed out, "Tish!" at the same time that Mom screamed out, "Ray!" The tree fell over behind me and all the Christmas lights went out at once.

All could think was, Matt's not supposed to see this. He's not supposed to think Santa Claus acts this way.

Mom started pleading with Dad—to ignore me, I think—and Dad started yelling back, and then they were outside, yelling at each other so loud the neighbors had to have heard. I heard Dad say, "I know when I'm not wanted," and then I heard his truck start. And then all we could hear was Mom crying.

And that's been it, he hasn't been back at all. Mom told me yesterday at breakfast, "Well, you drove him off. He left town again." I don't know how she knows—from some of his buddies down at the Alibi Inn, I guess. But she hasn't said anything else to me, just looks at me real angry and tightlipped.

Matt looks at me kind of mad-like too, sometimes. He's still confused. I've tried to talk to him, to tell him I didn't mean to make Dad go away, to tell him I'd like it, too, if Dad were around all the time, being nice all the time, but that's just not how things are. Matt nods his head and says, "Uh-huh," when I ask him if he understands and, "Huh-uh," when I ask if he's upset with me. I know he doesn't understand, though. I know he spends almost as much time crying as Mom does.

If Granma were still alive, she would understand. She would tell me I did the right thing. I think. Or would she be mad at me, too?

It's strange how it's such a relief now to go to work at the Burger Boy. I don't have to think at all there, just punch in the orders and wipe down the tables and pull the French fries and onion rings out of the fryer when the buzzer goes off. I went over Bud's head and asked Mr. Seagrave to schedule me for as many hours as possible over break. Nobody else wants to work, so I'm getting almost thirty hours this week.

Tish,

Okay. Your first three entries are rather short, but your last one more than makes up for that. I'm impressed that you were inspired to write during the break! That shows a real commitment as a journal-keeper!

JANUARY 12

Don't read this, Mrs. Dunphrey.

Yeah, right, I am such a committed journal-keeper. Thank you very much for the compliment. It makes the rest of my life okay. (Not.)

Home still stinks. Bud's being mean to me at work, making me scrub the bathrooms every two hours. And at school—finals are this week, and I'm screwing up bad. I just can't concentrate. I even tried to study, but it just makes me do worse. I sat down with my biology book last night, and I ended up staring at the same page for two hours. Mom had the TV on too loud—all I could hear was laugh tracks. It didn't make me feel like laughing.

JANUARY 15

Don't read, Mrs. Dunphrey.

Everything stinks. Why should I care?

I think Matt hates me now. He cries all the time and keeps asking, "When's Daddy coming back?"

Last night, I told him, "Look, you're eight years old. Quit acting like a baby. Grow up."

It didn't help.

But he is eight. Why can't he be tougher?

Oh, yeah, in other great news . . . I think I flunked the geometry final today. And Rochelle is mad at me because I won't let her fix me up with this total skag, Billy Rogers.

JANUARY 20

Don't read this, Mrs. Dunphrey.

You know how sometimes, it's rainy and dreary for weeks, it seems, and everybody gets depressed and snappy because the skies are always gray—and then one day the sun finally comes out and it seems so great, you think, "I'll never be unhappy again"? That's exactly how I feel today.

Everything has been so bad since Christmas, I haven't even noticed whether the sun's shining or not. Mom's still not really speaking to me—that's still bad—but last night, Matt came up when I was watching this old Dracula movie on TV. He cuddled against me and he said, "You're a good sister. I know *you'll* never leave me like Daddy and Granma did."

I started to tell him it wasn't fair to put Daddy and Granma in the same category—I mean, Granma died. But it was so nice to have him not mad at me, I didn't say anything. He kind of leaned his head on my shoulder and we watched the rest of the movie together. It was so old, it wasn't scary at all, just funny. You could see the wires holding things up. And I know the castle in the background was cardboard, because it almost fell over once or twice. Matt and I laughed and laughed and laughed. Mom was at work, or maybe we could have gotten her laughing, too.

Then today, Rochelle told me I was right about Billy Rogers being a jerk, and she wished she was as smart as I was about men. (!)

And you know what else? I did better than I thought on

all my finals. Even the geometry one was just a D, not an F. My semester grades are all C's. (Hey, I know I shouldn't be excited about C's, but the thought of taking anything over again, or during summer school, was really making me sick.)

JANUARY 22

Don't read this, Mrs. Dunphrey.

Oops. I totally forgot about this being due today.

It's funny, I was writing on Wednesday about how good people feel when the sun comes out. Well, we've got this weird heat wave going on right now—it's really sunny and almost hot. People came to school without their coats—I mean, in January!—and the radio said it was going to be in the high fifties today. Chastity told me Mike Bryant was wearing shorts in her history class, but Mr. Tremont told him it wasn't June yet, and he had to go put on his sweatpants from gym.

Tish,

This is all right, but your entries seem to be getting shorter. Try to regain your habit of writing so wonderfully extensively here.

JANUARY 27

DON'T read this, Mrs. Dunphrey.

Yes, ma'am, I will try to begin writing so "wonderfully extensively" again. I'm so sorry I lost my journal-keeping commitment for a while there. I should have remembered that that was supposed to be the most important thing in my life.

Do you know how dumb this is? What good is this journal, anyway? It's not like I'm ever going to be a writer or anything. And it's not like anybody would ever care about my life, that they'd ever read this (or that I'd ever let anyone read this). If any adult really cared about me, my life would be totally different, let me tell you. That's why I'm trying so hard to make things better for Matt. Not that I'm doing too great a job at it.

But about school—it's just silly, the stupid little assignments all you teachers make up. And then Mrs. Rachethead takes five points off anything if we forget to tear off the scraggly edges of our paper where it comes out of wire notebooks. And Mr. Tremont won't accept our homework unless we've got our name, the date, the class, and the page numbers, in that order, in the upper right-hand corner of every page. Do you all make up these rules just to amuse yourselves? Just to jerk our chains?

The thing is, I kind of like you, Mrs. Dunphrey. You were probably a brain or something when you were in high school—how else did you end up being a teacher?—but I could kind of see how if we were the same age, we might be friends. You do have cool clothes, even if you don't have very big bangs. And you pretty much treat us kids like human beings, not like mutants or something. I mean, maybe you're just real good at acting, but when you talk to students, you really do seem to listen. I heard how, when Carrie Roderick and Jason Bly broke up, and Carrie was in tears all day, you took her out in the hall and talked to her. She told everyone you couldn't have been nicer.

But with all that, why can't you see how stupid all this school stuff is? I may not be working at Burger Boy the rest of my life (God, I hope not) but it won't be at a job much better. When is it ever going to matter if I know anything else?

JANUARY 29

Don't read this, Mrs. Dunphrey.

Guess I got a little carried away on Wednesday. It's just hard to get concerned about school when Mom is acting so totally freaked out.

Honestly, she was acting so weird last night I almost asked her if she was taking some kind of drugs. Her eyes were all glassy, and she wouldn't say anything to Matt or me. I asked her all sorts of questions—did she want me to get her something to eat? Was the heat high enough for her? Did she want me to get her a pan of water to soak her feet in? (They hurt all the time from standing at the cash register.) But she didn't answer anything. Finally her friend Brenda from work called, and when I handed her the phone, she did say an "uh-huh" or "huh-uh" or two.

Then after she said good-bye, she kept holding the phone, cuddling it almost.

"Mom, you want me to hang that up for you?" I asked her. The phone company's computer voice was coming on every few seconds, saying, "Your phone is off the hook."

I don't think she even heard it, or me. But she did say something to me, for practically the first time since Christmas.

"He does love me, I know he does."

I wanted to say, "Yeah, that's why he uses you as his own personal punching bag." But I didn't. I can't help feeling a little guilty about making Dad leave, if Mom wanted him around so bad. So I said, "Yeah, Mom, I know. He loves you a lot. He just has a lot of problems."

I tried saying that like I meant it, to try and cheer Mom up. But you know, when I got to thinking about it, maybe it was true. I've seen Dad look at Mom like he thinks she's hot stuff. But if you want to talk about being messed up, it's like my parents are competing. I don't know how many jobs Dad has had and lost—and to hear him talk, it's never his fault. Maybe, sometimes, it isn't. I mean, lots of other kids' parents are out of work, too. They keep telling us at school that you can't get a good job without a lot of education, because so many of the factories around here have closed down—even the place Granpa used to work, that made aerosol cans. That shut down a long, long time ago. And it's not like Dad even has his high school diploma. He and Mom both dropped out when she got pregnant with me.

Great. We're back to everything being my fault.

Anyhow, it didn't do any good for me to try and be nice to Mom. After I said that, she didn't say anything at all, just sat there staring. Finally I tugged the phone out of her hand, because I wanted to call Sandy. Mom didn't move, even then. She kept her fingers curled like she still had something to hold on to.

Maybe I should talk to Brenda, ask her if Mom acts normal at work. But I don't know if I can trust Brenda. I think she's the one who kept telling Mom to go to the Alibi Inn all the time to find out about Dad—and to find Dad, when he was actually there. I think Brenda is dating one of Dad's friends or something, and she's been telling Mom where Dad is now.

Really, Brenda seems as bad as Sandy or Rochelle or Chastity about guys. Just once I'd like to know a grown-up who really acts grown up.

I guess that's why I miss Granma so much. She was a lot older than Brenda or Mom, of course, but it was like she'd really learned something in all her years. She wasn't out chasing guys like some fifteen-year-old. She'd say things like, "If you don't respect yourself, how do you expect anyone else to?" I think Dad really hated her, but there wasn't anything he could do, because we were staying at her house. One time, I remember, she told him she was going to call the police on him if he didn't leave Mom and us kids alone. And he did. That time. After that, I think he figured out she really wouldn't call the police, because she didn't want anyone to know how bad things were at her house.

She told me once that her failing was pride. I didn't know

what she meant then, but maybe that's what she was talking about.

Except, she'd also send me off to school saying, "Make me proud today, Tish!" like pride was something good.

You know, I did do really well in school before Granma died.

FEBRUARY 1

Don't read this, Mrs. Dunphrey.

It's kind of a nothing day today. Mom's still being weird, school still stinks, the Burger Boy is still boring. I'm sorry, Mrs. Dunphrey, I just can't write tons when nothing is happening. Sometimes I think maybe I'll wake up one morning and life will be totally different—everything will be good . . . My parents will be normal, Matt won't be so whiny, I'll have plenty of money without working at the Burger Boy, I'll have great clothes, I won't have to go to school, I'll have a boyfriend who's really nice to me (hey, this is just a dream) . . . And let's see, since this is just a dream—Granma will still be alive. Wouldn't it be great?

But I keep waking up every morning to the same old life.

Bummer.

FEBRUARY 4

Don't read this, Mrs. Dunphrey.

I have a new way of dealing with Mom: I just ignore her.

I figure, she's the adult here, not me, so why should I try to baby her? For a while there, I was acting like she was Matt—like it was my responsibility to take care of her. But if she wants to act like Zombie Queen of the Universe, that's her problem, not mine.

Now it's kind of like Matt and I have our lives, and then there's this other presence in the house that's just barely there. I try not to even notice if she's sitting in the living room watching TV, or not, when I come home from school or the Burger Boy. I still walk Matt home from school, I still try to make sure he has enough to eat, I still clean up the kitchen once or twice a week. I talk to him all the time, but I don't even try with Mom. Last night Matt was playing with his Matchbox cars on the living-room floor and I decided I wanted to watch *Rescue 911* instead of *Wheel of Fortune*, which was on. I asked Matt if he minded if I turned the channel, but I didn't even think about Mom until Matt asked her if she cared. And she was sitting right there.

She just grunted, anyhow. Nothing matters to her except Dad.

The weird thing is, life doesn't really seem that different than it was before I was ignoring Mom. It's not like she's really said anything to me since Christmas except, "He does love me. I know he does," that one day, and, "How could you? Yelling at your own father . . ." a couple of other times. Maybe if she'd yelled at me, it would have made sense. But she just whined and backed off when I defended myself.

How can my mother be such a wimp?

I bet Granma was really ashamed of her. She just must not have let it show around Matt and me.

Tish,

Looks fine. You really have written a lot this time.

FEBRUARY 12

DON'T YOU DARE READ THIS, Mrs. Dunphrey.

It's four in the morning, and I'm writing here because I can't sleep at all. I lie on my front, then my side, then my back, then my front again . . . And all the time my brain's racing around thinking of new things to worry about.

I'm scared. I'm scared like I've never been before. Mom's gone.

I got home from working at the Burger Boy tonight about nine o'clock, and I was kind of surprised because the whole house was dark. I knew Matt had to be home, and I was pretty sure Mom wasn't supposed to go in to work until midnight.

Then the first thing I heard when I unlocked the front door was Matt sniffling. I swear, he was back in his room, hiding under his bed, but he was crying so loud you could hear him all through the house. I yelled out, "Matt, what's wrong?"—I mean, I was thinking maybe someone had broken in and beaten him and robbed us. Or something like that, not that there'd be anything to steal in our house. I even called out, "Mom?" forgetting I was ignoring her. But Matt didn't answer, and Mom sure didn't.

I turned on the light in the living room, and there weren't any signs that anyone had broken in. And that's when I saw the note on the coffee table.

I've got it memorized now:

TISH,

I'VE GONE TO FIND YOUR FATHER. I KNOW YOU'LL

TAKE CARE OF MATT WHILE I'M AWAY.

MOM

The weird thing is, at first, I couldn't make myself understand it. It's like I could read, but I didn't know what the words meant. Then I was like, "Oh, Mom's gone to find Dad. Well, maybe that's better than having her sitting around here bawling all the time."

Then I read the note again. And again. She didn't say anything about coming back. Did she mean she wasn't? I read the note one more time, but there's not a whole lot to figure out from those two sentences. I have to admit, I felt a little lightheaded. It's not like Mom was ever Mother-of-the-Year material, but no one wants their mother to run away.

And then I thought, did I drive her away because I was ignoring her? Or—is it my fault anyhow, because it's my fault Dad left?

Matt snuck up behind me then and grabbed me around the waist. He held on so tight I could hardly breathe.

"Mom's gone," he said. He looked terrible—hair all messed up, eyes all puffy from crying, lint all over his shirt.

"Yeah, she's gone," I said. "So what? What'd she ever do when she was here?"

I sounded really mean, because I was scared, I guess. He started crying harder, like I'd hit him or something.

"Hey, don't cry," I said. "I'm not saying I didn't like Mom. But we'll do okay without her. That's all."

"Will she come back?"

"I don't know. Don't count on it. Then you'll be happy if she does. Okay? In the meantime—you know I'll never leave you."

That seemed to make him feel better.

"She left us some money, didn't she?" he asked.

I hadn't even thought of that. We went over to the kitchen drawer where Mom always keeps an envelope of money. It was empty, of course.

"It doesn't matter," I said. "I make lots of money at the Burger Boy. I'll take care of everything."

I kept talking to Matt like that—telling him how good everything was going to be, how I'd take care of him and it'd be like an adventure, just him and me. And by the time I got him to brush his teeth and crawl into bed, he was even giggling.

Then I came back to my room, and I started thinking about how I don't make enough money at the Burger Boy to take care of everything. I don't even know what bills Mom has to pay. Do they come in the mail, or do you have to go to the electric company and stuff to pick them up?

I told myself, maybe Mom will be back tomorrow, and all this will be silly.

But I couldn't really believe it, you know?

I probably sat on my bed, worrying, for about an hour. And then I did something really strange. I dug back on the floor of my closet and pulled out the old, mashed afghan

Granma had me working on before she died. The crochet hook was on the closet floor, too, under some old T-shirts, and I figured out how to put it in the yarn and crochet. I had to really concentrate—in, loop, out, loop, out, out—I'm surprised I remembered at all. The afghan smelled a little bit like the lavender soap Granma used to use. But I didn't really think about that while I was crocheting. I didn't think about anything for a long time. It was kind of comforting.

I don't know how long I crocheted, but eventually I had to stop. And then I started worrying again.

Why didn't Granma teach me something smart, like paying bills, instead of how to crochet?

FEBRUARY 15

DON'T read this, Mrs. Dunphrey.

Mom's still not back. I think I was right—she is gone for good.

What I'm scared of most is that someone will find out. Last Friday, when I first saw Mom's note, there was a part of me that wanted to call one of my friends—Chastity, probably, because when you come right down to it, she's the nicest—and tell her everything and ask her what to do. I'm so glad I didn't, though. She would have been all nice and sympathetic on the phone, or maybe told me everything was great—"Hey, that means you won't have anyone to boss you around? What's the problem?" But then the minute I'd hang up, she'd be on the phone to Rochelle or Sandy or someone else, saying, "You'll never guess what happened to Tish. Her parents are so screwed up . . ." It'd be embarrassing. Everybody in the whole school would know the next day.

And then things could get even worse. I didn't even think about what could happen if adults knew. But today at lunch Rochelle started telling about this freshman—Cashaundra Somebody—whose parents died in a car crash over the weekend. This Cashaundra has three or four brothers and sisters, and there weren't any relatives to take care of the kids, so they all got split up and put in different foster homes.

Matt and I don't have any relatives to take care of us, either. Granma and Granpa are both dead, and Dad's mom and dad moved away a long time ago. I think they disowned Dad or something. (Who can blame them?) I don't ever remember even meeting them. And if they don't even care enough to meet me and Matt, you think they're going to want to take care of us? So it'd be foster homes for Matt and me, too. If anybody tried to split us up—I'd kill them.

I'm so glad I was smart enough to tell Matt not to tell anyone—not his friends, his teacher, anybody—that Mom was gone.

I don't think he has any friends, anyhow. I just hope he doesn't let it slip to his teacher.

FEBRUARY 17

DON'T read this, Mrs. Dunphrey.

All week I've been real jumpy, scared someone would find out, scared some bill would come I couldn't pay, scared of everything. But it's weird, life is going on just fine without Mom.

Last night I got the nerve to call Mom's friend Brenda, to kind of feel her out and see if she knew anything. I pulled this trick we used to play on people back in junior high—I pretended she was the one who called me, and I was just talking to be polite. Back in junior high, Sandy used to be real good at confusing people, doing that. I remember she made Jenny Marlin cry one time with that trick. I wasn't sure Brenda was dumb enough to fall for it, but it worked. (I think she'd been drinking when I called.) What I got out of Brenda was this: Mom quit her job at Haggarty's, but she told everyone it was just because she got a better job somewhere else. (Yeah, right. She's lucky she never got fired at Haggarty's, the way she kept taking sick days.) Last Brenda heard, Dad was somewhere out west, California, maybe. Brenda didn't know anything about Mom going to find him. She just thought Mom had gone kind of snobby since she got this other job.

The funny thing is, right before we were hanging up, Brenda said to me, "Well, I just called to tell your mom she shouldn't forget all of us at Haggarty's, just because she's making twice the money now. Tell her to stop in and say 'hi' sometime, if she wants to keep her friends."

Am I good, or what?

Guess I have to give Mom some credit for fooling Brenda, too. Except, Brenda's a pretty dim bulb.

At least I know now for sure—or pretty sure—that nobody's out there nosing around, finding out about Mom leaving us, wanting to split Matt and me up.

Tish,

You only have three entries this time, but your first one is so exceptionally long that I'll give you full credit, anyhow. Try to write four entries next time, okay?

FEBRUARY 23

DO NOT read this, Mrs. Dunphrey.

I've been so scared.

I handed this in on Friday, and then the next period it hit me—how could I have been so dumb? I was trying so hard to keep it secret that Mom had left, and then I'd given Mrs. Dunphrey this notebook, with an exact description of everything, of Mom leaving, of me trying to take care of Matt, of me worrying about the bills. Everything. I know she's not supposed to be reading this, but what if, just this once, she had?

Sitting in history class, I got to feeling so panicky, I started sweating. Chastity leaned over and asked me if I needed to go to the nurse.

And then Mrs. Dunphrey handed this back today, with just the note about how many entries I had. Like that matters.

For a while, I was thinking I just wouldn't write any more in here, or I'd stop handing it in, or something.

But you know, it does make me feel a little better to write, since I can't talk to anyone. I mean, I can talk to Matt about Mom being gone, but I always have to be cheerful around him or he'll start crying. So maybe I will keep writing. I don't know. It's not the biggest thing on my mind right now.

I've been trying not to spend any money since Mom left, because I'm scared we're not going to have enough. I told Sandy and Rochelle and Chastity I was going on a diet, so they won't ask questions when I don't get anything to eat for lunch. But then Rochelle said, "At least get a Diet Coke out of the pop machine—hey, get me one, too." And then Sandy and Chastity wanted some, too, and you know they didn't pay me for it. So I had to spend almost three dollars—more than I would have spent on lunch.

Three dollars may not sound like much, but that's almost a whole hour of work at the Burger Boy. How much is the heat bill going to be? How much is the phone bill? What other bills am I going to have to pay?

Then Matt came home with this note about how his class is going to some field trip, and he needed a permission slip signed and five dollars for admission to the museum and lunch while they're there. I can forge Mom's signature, no problem, but I couldn't find more than $4.50 to give him, not even after looking for change in the couch after he went to bed.

FEBRUARY 24

Don't read this, Mrs. Dunphrey.

I was ready to kill Matt tonight. We were watching MTV together, when that news guy, Kurt Loder, started talking about how much money all the big singers have. It was making me a little sick—what's so great about, say, Madonna, that she has millions and millions of dollars while I'm wondering if Matt and I are even going to have enough money for groceries next week? But Matt started giggling and said, "With Mom's money, we're about as rich as them, aren't we?"

"In your dreams," I said, and threw one of Granma's crocheted pillows at him. "You saw that empty envelope."

"No, really," Matt said. "That was a big check Mom left, wasn't it?"

"What are you talking about?" I sat up straight. Matt gets confused about things sometimes, but he really seemed to think Mom left us something besides a note. Because Matt's been so scared of everything, I've been very careful not to mention money or anything else I'm worried about. But now I wanted to grab him by the shirt and hold his face up to my face and stare him right in the eye, just like people always do in the movies when they want important information.

"I tried to tell you, but you said you had enough money from Burger Boy. Then after that I thought you knew—didn't you?" Matt gave me a quick, nervous glance. "Mom didn't pick up her paycheck, you were supposed to. I think there were some other checks, too . . ."

I took a deep breath. I didn't explode like I wanted to. I started asking Matt really, really easy questions. After about a half hour, I finally got the whole story:

I guess Mom was still here when Matt got home from school the day she left. He was hungry and started looking for the new groceries—Mom usually goes shopping on Fridays, right after work, because that's her payday. But he couldn't find anything. So he asked Mom and she said she'd forgotten to pick up her paycheck. He started bugging her to go to the grocery right then, but she ignored him, so he went to play in his room. After a while, she came in and kissed him and said, "Good-bye. I forgot to write this down—tell Tish to pick up my paycheck and ask for all my vacation money, too." Matt figured Mom was just going to the grocery.

"Didn't you think at all?" I couldn't help saying. "Why would Mom write something? Why would she want me to pick up her check if she was going to Haggarty's?"

I was suddenly so mad I could barely see—here I'd been worrying so much about money when we had lots of it all along. How could Matt have gone almost two weeks without telling me? I was mad at him, too, because he didn't figure things out and stop Mom from leaving—I mean, she never would have kissed him if she was just going down to Haggarty's. And I think I was mad because Mom did that to Matt, acting like she was just going to the store, when she was actually leaving us. And maybe a little of my mad was because Mom didn't even kiss me, just left that stupid note.

But it didn't do me any good to yell, because as soon as I did, Matt's lower lip started trembling and his eyes got all watery.

"I'm not smart like you," he said. He blinked and that made the tears spill out onto his cheeks.

"Okay, okay." I had to take another deep breath and remind myself it wasn't Matt's fault Mom left. "I'm just glad you're telling me about this now. You're sure Mom said that about the vacation money?"

Matt nodded. "So we are rich?"

I rolled my eyes. But I was done being mad. So Mom did leave some money for us. Maybe she's not so bad after all. She must be planning to come home before the money runs out, right?

FEBRUARY 25

Don't read, Mrs. Dunphrey.

I was so excited about Mom's checks I decided to skip school this morning to go pick them up. I wrote out a long, long grocery list and was going to buy things like Snickers and Coco-Puffs as special treats for Matt and me. I waltzed into Haggarty's like I owned the world. But guess what? Mom called in sick so much they said she'd run out of sick days and used up all her vacation days, and then some. So they didn't owe her anything.

Except—I don't know. The assistant manager may have been lying just because he didn't want to give me Mom's checks. The first thing he told me was that Mom's the only one "authorized" to pick up her paychecks. He didn't tell me that thing about the sick days until I started yelling. And then, everything I said, he kept saying, "Really, it's not appropriate for me to discuss this with anyone but your mother." I was so mad. I wanted so bad to yell, "Oh yeah? What if she's in California?" But of course I couldn't.

I hate Mom. I don't care if she ever comes back.

FEBRUARY 26

Don't read this, Mrs. Dunphrey.

I went to pick Matt up after school today, and he was slow coming out, so I had a long time to stand there watching all the other kids. They all looked so happy, dressed in all sorts of bright colors, laughing and talking to each other. And then Matt came out, pretty much at the last. His coat is dull gray, one I got for him at Goodwill last fall. He hadn't buttoned it at all, and it was kind of falling off his one shoulder because it's a little big for him. His shirt had come untucked from his pants, and his pants had holes in both knees. His hair was sticking out all over the place, like he hadn't combed it in about three days.

He looked like one of those kids everybody picked on when I was in grade school, and like he might cry at any minute.

He looked like some kid nobody loved.

I'd planned to make macaroni and cheese or something and just spend all night at home, or maybe leave Matt at home while I went to a party with Rochelle. But when I saw how awful Matt looked, I decided I had to do something special. We walked home and I told him to take a bath and put on his best clothes. I called Rochelle and told her, forget the party, I was sick. I put on this dress that Mom insisted on me buying a year ago for some neighbor's funeral—I mean, me, in a dress?—and then I took Matt over to the Burger Boy and told him to order anything he wanted. (I got paid yesterday—at least I get paid, unlike Mom.) I told him we were celebrating being on our own. "See?" I said. "I told you we could get along just fine without Mom and Dad."

Just talking about it made him get all sniffly, but I quick changed the subject and started telling him jokes about talking cows and friendly robots and any sort of nonsense I could make up. After a while he was laughing with me. I pretended to fly French fries around his head before parking them in his mouth. He laughed a lot at that. The other customers at the Burger Boy were looking at us like we were happier than them. And then when we were leaving, Lexy Samuels, who was behind the counter tonight, asked me, "Is that your little brother? He's really cute." He did look really cute then. He'd even slicked his hair back like that kid in the *Home Alone* movies.

Then I almost ruined the whole thing when we got home and Matt showed me this picture he'd drawn for school. He said the teacher had told them to draw their family, and Matt had just drawn himself and a picture of a bigger girl with lots of brown hair—me—standing outside a white house. It was a good picture—the kids even kind of looked like Matt and me—but it was like advertising, "Our mother and father left us."

"You didn't draw Mom?" I said. "Did the teacher ask you why not?"

I almost went crazy when Matt said, "Yes."

"So what'd you say?" I asked, trying not to panic.

"I told her we were at our Granma's, and she was in the house waiting to take care of us," he said. "Was that wrong?"

I told him that was a good answer, and I hugged him and hugged him so he'd know I wasn't mad.

FEBRUARY 28

Don't read this, Mrs. Dunphrey.

It's really late, and I can't sleep again, for worrying. All these bills have started coming in the mail—even more than I thought. I mean, I didn't even know people had to pay for water, and the city wants almost $20 just for that.

Almost all the bills say they don't have to be paid until the middle of next month. I hope I can figure out something by then. Maybe Mom will even come back before then. (Yeah, right.)

At least one of the bills, the one for Mom's credit card, kind of solved a mystery. Guess what? All those big presents Dad got us—even that dinner at Shoney's—he put on Mom's credit card. I bet he's the one who took Mom's "missing" Christmas money, too. What a nice guy, huh? There were lots of other things on the bill, too—lots of bar tabs at the Alibi Inn that I know were Dad's, not Mom's, because Mom can't drink more than one beer without falling asleep. And it looks like the card was maxed out the day after Christmas. So Dad just left when he couldn't use Mom's card anymore. It wasn't my fault at all.

At least, that's what I want to think. If it's not my fault Dad left, it's not my fault Mom left, either.

So why do I still feel guilty every time I see how sad Matt looks? Why do I feel like I deserve to have all these problems—keeping everything secret, not having enough money, always worrying about Matt?

Everything's so screwed up.

I crocheted a little bit more on the old afghan tonight after Matt went to bed. It's strange how that makes me feel better. Some, anyway. I guess it's about the only thing I have left to remind me of Granma.

For some reason, I've been thinking a lot lately about the day she died. It was summertime, and I was out in this vacant lot behind our house playing hide-and-go-seek with this neighbor girl, Misty Tyler. I heard Mom in the house scream out, "Help! Somebody! Call an ambulance!"

I got up and ran inside, and Misty yelled, "Wait! I didn't find you yet!"

By the time I got to the house, one of the neighbors had gotten Mom calmed down and called an ambulance. I shoved my way back to Granma's room—it's Matt's room now—and she was lying on the floor, not moving. It's weird. I hadn't seen Granma fall or anything, but I could picture just how it would be, her legs going limp like a piece of yarn, her falling sideways until her knees, her hips, her elbows, then her head hit the ground.

I don't know, maybe it had happened before.

This time, I stood there saying, "Granma, Granma, Granma," until finally she opened her eyes.

"Tish," she kind of whispered. "Find—find Matt."

I went back to my room—Matt and I shared then—and he was hiding under the bed. By the time I got him pulled out, the ambulance people were there and they kept saying, "Out of the way, kids." So I didn't get to see Granma again. Mom called us from the hospital that night and told us Granma was dead.

It's so odd. Before Granma died, I wouldn't have said I felt safe. I wouldn't have said I felt good about my life. But after she died, it seemed like if she was just alive again, everything would be fine.

It's like I'd been walking a tightrope with a big safety net underneath me, but I never really thought about the net until someone took it away. And then every single step scared me to death.

Maybe I keep thinking about Granma dying now to remind myself—it was worse to have her die than to have Mom leave.

MARCH 5

Don't read this, Mrs. Dunphrey.

This is due next period, so I have about forty-five minutes to decide whether I'm going to hand it in or not. It's such a crazy thing to worry about—I mean, I've never in my life done homework for any reason except to hand it in. (And a lot of times, I don't even do it then! Ha, ha.) I just don't want Mrs. Dunphrey "accidentally" reading this. I could be like Sandy and just skip it. But I keep telling Matt to act normal, like nothing's changed, so no one gets suspicious. I've always handed this journal in. If I don't, will Mrs. Dunphrey start being nosy?

I wish I could decide something. Why do even stupid things like this have to be hard now?

MARCH 9

Don't read this, Mrs. Dunphrey.

Oh, great, that was really bright of me. I decided not to hand this in, so of course Mrs. Dunphrey had to ask me to stay after class on Monday. She started doing this whole concerned-teacher routine, about how she realized I could be a little, uh, erratic with my work at times, but I'd always been faithful handing in my journal—was there something wrong? Was there anything I wanted to talk about?

I gave her this big story about how, silly me, I'd just forgotten to hand the notebook in on Friday, and I didn't remember until Saturday, when I saw it still in my stack of schoolbooks on my desk at home. I gave her the notebook and flipped through the pages for her—real quick, so she couldn't read anything—and she said, wow, you really did write a lot. Six entries! And almost all of them extremely long!

I must say, I was a great liar, I acted so worried that I'd forgotten to hand it in when I had done all the work. Mrs. Dunphrey ended up telling me she'd give me partial credit, because I had written so much, but she had to take off something for it being late. Then she gave me this little lecture about how she was sure I was capable of much better work than I was actually doing in her class . . .

Geez, Mrs. Dunphrey, chill. How can you care so much about something as stupid as this journal? Or my grades? I mean, you're lucky I even bother to show up for class. School ranks about 1,001 on my list of concerns.

I've been thinking lately, maybe the answer to all Matt's and my money problems is for me to drop out of school. What am I getting out of school, anyhow? All this time I'm sitting in worthless classes, I could be earning money. I sure don't love my job at the Burger Boy, but if I went to full-time there, I wouldn't have to worry so much about the bills. It seems like every single one of them is due next week. What happens if they don't get paid? Would the electric company shut off our heat? It's been really cold lately. I mean, Matt and I could freeze.

MARCH 11

Don't read this, Mrs. Dunphrey.

Do you know how stupid the world is?

I went in to Mr. Seagrave this afternoon, and told him what I wrote about Tuesday—I mean, I sure didn't say I was worried about paying the bills because Mom left us, but I did say I wasn't getting anything out of school and I was thinking about dropping out so I could work full-time at the Burger Boy. He got this real serious look on his face and said, "Tish, you can't do that."

That made me mad right off—I was expecting this big lecture about how no one should drop out of school. I was ready to say that what I did with my life was my own business, and if I wanted to drop out, that was my problem, not his. But he didn't say anything about how it was bad to drop out of school. Instead, he said Burger Boy had a policy that it wouldn't hire people without high school diplomas.

Wait a minute, I said, I don't have a diploma, and I've been working here since I turned fifteen.

And then he explained how that was different—obviously teenagers working part-time wouldn't have their diplomas. But for adult full-time employees, Burger Boy expected a certain level of educational achievement, and that level included, at the very least, a high school diploma.

I couldn't help getting smart-alecky. I think I said something like, how would a high school diploma help me flip burgers? Since when does it take twelve years of school to know how to clean a toilet?

I have to say, Mr. Seagrave was real patient He never once resorted to that adult trick of saying, "You'll understand when you're older." I think he knows the rules are stupid, too.

But none of this solves our problems.

Tonight I yelled at Matt for leaving the light on in his room while he was in the living room watching TV. We can't pay for all that energy, I told him. I got him so scared he started to cry.

And then I felt bad. What's one light matter? With what I've saved out of my Burger Boy checks since last month, we can barely pay the $20 water bill, let alone anything else. We might as well enjoy ourselves. I told Matt go ahead, turn everything on. I went around flipping switches—I turned on all our lights, all our radios, everything electric. I even turned on the fan, even though it's freezing outside.

That little tantrum scared Matt, too. He just cried harder.

I don't know what to do. If I didn't have to act grown up for Matt, I think I'd cry, too.

MARCH 15

Don't read this, Mrs. Dunphrey.

I called the electric company today, and made up this story about how I'd just lost my job and I wasn't going to be able to pay my bill this month. I didn't give my name or anything, and I tried to sound like a grown-up. I got transferred about six times, until finally I got some kind of caseworker. She asked why I wasn't getting unemployment (I said, "I don't know"—pretty dumb answer, huh?) and then she started giving me the names of all these agencies and stuff that could help me. She was all ready to arrange appointments for me. She kept asking my name so she could make the appointments. I was getting pretty panicked and was about to hang up—I started thinking, what if they trace their calls? It happens on TV all the time. Then suddenly she put me on hold for a minute, and someone else picked up the phone. I told my made-up story again, and this time the woman said, "Honey, I'm not supposed to be telling people this, but I know how things can be. If you just send in any money—five dollars, say—that establishes what we call an intent to pay, and we won't cut off service. Then when you're back on your feet, you can catch up your payments."

I was so happy, I probably told that woman "thank you" about sixty times. She practically had to hang up to get me to stop.

I have enough money to send five dollars for each of the bills. I hope the phone company and everyone else does things like the electric company. But the electric's the most important. It got down to fifteen degrees last night. Why can't it be warm?

I might as well ask, why can't I have normal parents who stay with their kids and take care of the bills themselves? Why can't Granma still be alive?

MARCH 17

Don't read this, Mrs. Dunphrey.

I sent back all the bills with the five dollars in each. Everything seems to be going okay now. It's even getting warmer. I forgot to wear green for Saint Patrick's Day, and

Roger Amway pinched me hard, but who cares? Matt was smart enough to remember what day it was, and he said nobody pinched him at school because he put some green marker on his hand.

Who needs Mom? Who needs Dad? We're doing fine, just Matt and me.

Tish,

Good. I'm glad you remembered to hand this in on time!

Would you mind letting me read one of your entries again soon?

MARCH 24

Don't read this, Mrs. Dunphrey.

I know, I know, you want to read another entry. But hey, I don't have the time to make up something else. I don't know why I bother writing in here at all. Except that now it kind of seems like this journal is my friend. And at the moment I really don't have any others.

Sandy and Rochelle are real mad at me. We got in this big fight at school on Friday because I said I couldn't go to the mall with them that night. They said all I do anymore is work or stay with Matt—"What's so exciting about an eight-year-old?" Sandy asked. Then Rochelle had to say something really mean: "Maybe Tish likes younger men." And Sandy said, "Maybe she's got something else going on—who is it, Tish? Roger Amway? Bud Turner? Both? How many guys are you screwing?"

I should have just walked away then—that's what Granma would have told me to do. But not me. I had to go and slug Sandy. She just makes me mad—her parents give her everything and she acts like it's nothing and then she goes and makes fun of me and Chastity because we don't have as nice clothes or anything . . .

Well, anyhow, I hit her pretty hard, and then she hit me back and Rochelle was kind of helping. Really, all Sandy did was scratch. She's such a sissy. But then she yelled out, loud enough for everyone in the cafeteria to hear, "Nobody'd screw you, you stink so bad."

"What do you mean?" I said.

"She means you stink," Rochelle said. "Pee-you. When was the last time you took a shower?"

I'd taken a shower that morning, but it was about the sixth time I'd worn my jeans and sweatshirt without washing them, because I never have time to do the laundry. (That was one thing Mom did do. Usually.) Do I really stink?

I didn't care then, I just wanted to shut Rochelle and Sandy up. I started hitting both of them at once, frantic-like, like some speeded-up cartoon character. They backed off a little, but not before Mr. Tremont came over saying, "What is this? A cat fight? Is there trouble in the gum-cracking brigade?" He acted like the whole thing was a joke. But he made all three of us go down to the office, and we all got a week's detention. So Matt has to walk home by himself all this week, and I had to get some of my hours changed at the Burger Boy. That means even less money.

Sandy and Rochelle still aren't talking to me, and I sure don't want to talk to them if they're going to be so mean. Since Chastity's been out sick all week, I don't have anyone to hang out with.

But you know what? It felt real good to haul off and hit Sandy and Rochelle. I wish I'd hit them each about ten more times.

MARCH 26

Don't read this, Mrs. Dunphrey.

Chastity's back at school now, and she made Sandy and Rochelle and me all apologize. I asked Chastity if she thought

I smelled bad, and she said of course not, that was just one of those things people say in a fight. I am going to do the laundry more often, though.

Sandy and Rochelle still aren't being real nice to me—they whisper all the time behind my back—but they will talk to me now. The only thing is, I had to agree to go with them to the mall tonight to get them to shut up about how I never do anything fun anymore. I was scheduled to work, so I called in sick. Bud took the call, and I know he didn't believe me.

I'm so stupid. I should have stayed mad at Sandy and Rochelle and asked for extra hours at Burger Boy. Right now, I need money more than friends.

Maybe I just won't eat next week.

MARCH 29

Don't read this, Mrs. Dunphrey.

When I was getting ready for school this morning, Matt came in and said he didn't have any clean underwear. I couldn't believe that, since I stayed up until 3 a.m. last night doing the laundry. I went into his room with him, and looked in his drawer, and he was right, there wasn't any underwear there. I asked him if he'd been putting his underwear in the dirty clothes basket. I tried to be nice about it, but I was so tired maybe I sounded mean . . . He started crying right off. That made me mad, and I wanted to hit him almost as bad as I'd wanted to hit Sandy last week. Why is Matt such a wimp?

After about fifteen minutes, he finally pointed under the bed. I crawled down there and sure enough, there was every bit of underwear Matt owns. I should have been able to smell it. Matt finally told me he'd been wetting his bed almost every night, but he was so ashamed he just hid the underwear. I looked at his sheets and they were all stained and stinky, too. It was gross. I blew up and yelled at Matt—why was he wetting his bed now? Didn't he know he was too old for that? Did he think I had time to change his sheets every night?

Matt just cried harder, and I got to feeling terrible. It's not like Matt is wetting his bed on purpose. I told him, to make it up to him, we'd both stay home from school, and I'd play games with him all day and fix him whatever he wanted for lunch, and we'd just have fun together.

I didn't remember until after school would have been out that I was supposed to have two tests today. It's not like I would have done very well on them, anyhow.

MARCH 30

Don't read this, Mrs. Dunphrey.

Matt and I didn't go to school today either. It felt so good just to sleep and sleep and sleep. I didn't get up until noon. Someone from Matt's school called to check up on him, but I just pretended to be Mom. I gave them some big story about how Matt had a horrible fever. And it wasn't really that much of a lie, because he does have a bad cold.

Nobody called from the high school to check up on me.

Today would have been as great as yesterday, except that, when I went to fix lunch for Matt and me, I couldn't find anything except Cheerios—no milk—and some icky kinds of soup that Mom must have bought for Dad. (Who else would eat something as sick as split pea?) So I guess I'll have to send Matt to school tomorrow so he'll get lunch. I don't get paid until Friday, and I'm all out of cash.

I decided to call the Burger Boy and see if I could get more hours. Guess what I found out? Mr. Seagrave got a new job somewhere else. That wouldn't matter so much except for who's going to replace him—good old Bud Turner. Gag, gag, gag. The person I talked to, Lexy, made some crack about how that would be great for me since Bud's always had a crush on me. I didn't tell her Bud's been real mean ever since I said I wouldn't go out with him. I hate the thought that he'll be my real boss, and I won't be able to go to Mr. Seagrave anymore.

APRIL 1

Don't read this, Mrs. Dunphrey.

Back when I was Matt's age, this was the day everyone was scared of—April Fool's Day. I never got tricked, but lots of people did. Mean tricks, too, like lids on catsup bottles being unscrewed so the next person who used them got a lapful of catsup.

When I saw the mail today, I expected someone to jump

out from somewhere and say, "Gotcha! April Fool's!"

But all the letters were real.

First, there were a ton more bills. It looks like Mom was playing that little five-dollar game herself with the electric company and the phone company and everybody else for a long time now. I got two bills today that said, "Final notice—pay in full or service will be cut off."

At least it's warmer outside now, so Matt and I won't freeze. Being without electricity can't be that bad, can it?

Anyhow, besides those bills, I got something that said "Notice of Property Tax." It's for something like $200, and when I read the fine print at the bottom, it said our house could be taken away if we don't pay.

Where am I supposed to get $200?

Then—and this really takes the cake—on top of all that, Mom sent us a postcard. It was of a beach somewhere in California, and she had written all about how she and Dad are back together now and happy, blah, blah, blah. At the bottom, it said, "Hope you and Matt are okay. I'll try to send some more money soon. You have enough for now, don't you? Love . . ."

Thanks, Mom. Thanks a lot. You'd better send that money fast, or the mailman will have to deliver it to us on the streets. And why'd you ask a question without a return address or phone number so we could answer?

I would have hidden the card from Matt, except he was the one who got the mail. Of course he started crying. And of course that made me mad and I yelled at him.

Sometimes I think maybe he'd be better off without me. I'm not taking very good care of him at all. His cold is worse, he's still wetting the bed, and he cries every day. But then tonight, he crawled up in my lap (even though he's really too big) and said he was glad I stayed with him.

After Matt was in bed, I crocheted a lot. But for once it didn't help me keep my mind off anything.

Anyhow, that stupid afghan is just about done.

Tish,

Wow—you did an extra entry again. Great! But can't you let me read one sometime soon?

APRIL 7

Don't read this, Mrs. Dunphrey.

Oops—I didn't mean to write five entries last time. At least Mrs. Dunphrey thinks I'm doing something right. Everything else is going wrong.

I got fired today.

The thing is, I didn't even do anything. When I went in to work, Bud told me he wanted to see me back in his office. And when I got there, he shut the door and said, "Tish, we're not going to need your help anymore."

I was real stupid—I kept saying, "What? What do you mean?"

He said since he'd taken over he'd found that the restaurant was definitely overstaffed, and he needed to let a few people go to keep the overhead low.

Yeah, right. Then why was I the only person fired?

I asked if he wanted me to work my regular shift tonight—I thought maybe I could be real nice to him and talk him into letting me keep my job. But Bud just said, "That won't be necessary." And then he gave me my last paycheck and told me good-bye.

He looked so happy firing me, I wish I'd punched him. Right in his pimply nose. But Granma would have been proud of me—I was real dignified. I said, "Fine. It's been a pleasure working with you."

If he could lie, so can I. I know he was just getting back at me for not going out with him back in the fall.

I haven't told anyone yet—I know Rochelle would tell me to file some sex discrimination suit or something. But I can't have anyone nosing around. And wouldn't I have to hire a lawyer for that?

Without my Burger Boy money, I can't afford anything.

Tomorrow I'm going to go look for another job. Wendy's has got to be hiring. Or McDonald's. Somebody.

APRIL 8

Don't read this, Mrs. Dunphrey.

I was wrong. Nobody is hiring. At least not now. I went to every fast-food restaurant in town—and don't think that's easy, when you have to go by city bus. I filled out probably twenty applications. Daddy-O's said they might be hiring in a month, and Hardee's said they might have some openings in the summer. But that was it. Great. What am I supposed to do until then?

Tomorrow I'll apply at other places. K-Mart. Wal-Mart. All the stores at the mall.

The thing is, who's going to hire me anyhow when they find out I was fired from my last job? It's not like Bud would give me a good recommendation.

Oh, one more thing—when I got home, the phone didn't work. I went next door and called the phone company, and the woman on the other end put me on hold forever and then came back on and said, "The reason your phone is out is that you're behind in your payment. When you pay your bill in full, we'll restore service. There is a $50 hook-up fee."

So even if any of these places want to hire me, they're not going to be able to call.

What am I going to do? I've only got $20 left from my last Burger Boy check, that property tax thing is due, and we don't have much food left.

I mean it. What am I going to do?

APRIL 12

Don't read this, Mrs. Dunphrey.

Matt and I just had Cheerios and peanut butter for supper tonight. That was all we had in the house. He went to bed crying because he said his stomach felt all squeezed-in and empty. And I think his cold isn't just a cold—I think it's the flu.

I've got to do something. I've got to.

APRIL 13

Don't you dare read this, Mrs. Dunphrey.

I'm not the least bit proud of this, but I shoplifted today for the first time in my life.

I went to Haggarty's, where Mom used to work. (I figured they owed us.) I stuffed a package of hamburger in my jacket before buying a loaf of bread and two candy bars. All those times watching Sandy shoplift must have paid off, because I didn't get caught. I was smart enough not to put the package in my jacket right in front of the meat case, because everyone knows the butchers look out through those windows. Nope, I put the hamburger in my cart, and went over to the canned vegetable aisle to cram the package into my top when no one was around.

Then, stupid me, I didn't pay attention to which checkout line I stood in, and ended up having Mom's friend Brenda check me out. She wanted to talk and talk and talk—she asked how Mom's new job was going and when Mom was going to actually call Brenda again. I had almost forgotten how Mom made up that story about getting a new job, so I almost gave everything away. And the whole time Brenda was asking me questions, the hamburger was slipping down inside my jacket. Finally I told her I had to go to work—hey, if you're going to steal, you might as well lie, too.

Once I got out of the store, I couldn't believe it. I felt free and trapped all at once. I whispered, "You're a criminal now." All I could think was, Granma would be so ashamed.

Then when I got home, and fixed the hamburger for Matt and me, I realized how dumb I was. If I was going to steal meat, why hadn't I stolen something really good, like steak?

At least Matt got a lot to eat tonight—three hamburgers. And there was enough left over so we'll have food for tomorrow night, too.

APRIL 15

Don't read this, Mrs. Dunphrey.

Matt and I are still eating hamburger. For some reason, it doesn't taste very good to me. I tell myself it's just because I had so many burgers at the Burger Boy, but I know that's not the reason.

Mrs. Dunphrey had me stay after class today so she could give me some big lecture about what a terrible student I've become. She asked me if I realized I'd been absent ten days in the past four weeks—I didn't know it was that much, but she's the one who's counting. I told her I'd been sick a lot. Really, a lot of those days, I stayed home with Matt because he was sick. Or some of those days, I was job-hunting. And, anyhow, I haven't felt much like going to school lately. But Mrs. Dunphrey was so suspicious I guess I'm going to have to. I don't want her calling in the truant officer or anything.

Then Mrs. Dunphrey asked if I understood that I can't pass the class without turning in my research paper. I guess it was due yesterday. I haven't even opened a book. But I gave her some big story about how I'd been working on the paper, but it wasn't quite done, and couldn't she please give me an extension. I don't think she believed me, but she was too nice to flat-out say, "You're lying." She did give me an extension, but it was like, "This is your last chance." I haven't turned in any work in any other class either, so why should English be any different? I *am* going to flunk this year. Why should I care?

Except, it kind of bothers me that Mrs. Dunphrey always

looks so disappointed whenever she sees me. I wish I could just say, "Look, Mrs. Dunphrey, here's why that paper doesn't matter to me. You want to hear about what my life's like?" It'd be such a relief to tell someone about Mom leaving. But then probably Mrs. Dunphrey'd tell someone else, and then where would Matt and me be?

No, I have to keep everything secret.

Tish,

Okay. I'm impressed that you have five entries again. Put some of that effort in on your research paper, too—all right?

APRIL 22

Don't read this, Mrs. Dunphrey.

I can't believe this happened—Sandy actually got caught shoplifting last night.

It was at this skaggy shop at the mall, Linda's Place. Sandy tried to put an orange minidress in her purse, and she got sloppy. The clerk saw the edge of the dress hanging out.

Rochelle was with her, and the security guards made both of them call their parents. (Geez, what would I have done if I'd been with Sandy? Say, "Uh, I don't know where my parents are, exactly"? That'd go over real well.)

Anyhow, the thing is, even though Sandy's dad is Mr. Bigtime Lawyer, both Sandy and Rochelle have to go to court now. Chastity told me they might even go to jail, but Sandy said nobody goes to jail for a first offense. Not for shoplifting, anyway.

Sandy's talking tough, but I think she's really scared. And Rochelle's totally freaked—she cried most of today. I don't think she ever thought she could get in trouble just for being with Sandy when Sandy shoplifted. Who'd have known?

I got real panicked hearing about the whole thing. Chastity thought I was just upset for Sandy, and she kept saying things like, "Well, we both knew she was going to get caught someday. Maybe it's better this way, so she'll stop doing it." (Of course she didn't say that while Sandy was around.) But Chastity only made me feel worse, because I was really thinking what if I had gotten caught shoplifting?

I had been planning to go to Haggarty's again tonight, and pick up something else. Now I'm too chicken.

Or, I don't know, maybe I would have been too chicken anyhow. Ever since I took that hamburger last week, I've felt bad. Dirty, almost. I'm no saint, but I always thought at least I was a better person than Sandy. Now, the only difference is—she got caught and I didn't.

Still. If I don't shoplift again, what are Matt and I going to eat now? I only have five dollars left, and we're both getting tired of peanut butter sandwiches.

I stopped in at all the places I'd applied for jobs, just in case someone had tried to call me. Nobody had. I just ended up wasting a lot of money on bus fare.

What's going to happen to Matt and me?

APRIL 26

Don't read this, Mrs. Dunphrey.

A notice arrived today about the property tax. I couldn't make sense of half of it—what's arrears, anyway?—but I think what it meant was that the city's going to own our house if we don't pay up right now.

So where are Matt and me supposed to live?

Maybe it will take a long time for the city to get around to taking our house. Sandy and Rochelle aren't going to court until June—Sandy said her dad said everything the government does takes forever. Maybe by the time the city's ready to take our house, I'll have a job and have enough money to pay. Or maybe Mom or Dad will come back. Or maybe we'll all wake up tomorrow and the world will be a perfect place. Yeah, right. I've got to do something, but I don't know what. I ran out of yarn for that stupid afghan, so I can't even do that to make myself feel better. It's probably big enough anyhow.

What am I going to do? I wish someone could tell me. What would Granma do?

Oh, who am I kidding? She's just a dead old lady who didn't know how to do anything but crochet.

APRIL 29

Don't read this, Mrs. Dunphrey.

When Matt and I got home from school tonight, we found out the electricity was shut off. I didn't even bother going next door to call. Nobody has to tell me we haven't been paying our bills.

I was going to walk down to the store on the corner to buy some candles, but then I remembered I don't have any money left. I searched through the whole house and finally found two old candles in the cabinet above the refrigerator. I think they're left over from the time we had that blizzard, when everyone's electricity was out for a week.

Anyhow, I tried to make a game of it with Matt, telling him we were going to pretend we were pioneers on the frontier, just the two of us, eating and everything by candlelight. He said he wanted to watch TV. And then when it got dark, he was scared of all the shadows the candles made on the walls. He said they looked like ghosts. Maybe I laid the pioneer story on too strong, talking about the wind and the wolves howling outside.

But he was so scared of the shadows—they kind of frightened me, too. The shadows flicker like the candles do. They're always jumping around. They could be ghosts. Nothing looks the same by candlelight.

I finally got Matt to just go to bed—I said he'd be in the dark then, regardless. And now I'm sitting up writing this, even though I've almost burnt down both the candles, and the shadows and the silence are really scaring me. I'm like Matt—I really would like the TV on. The radio, too. Anything.

I just stopped and tore out the last few rows of that old afghan, just so I could crochet them again. I needed to do something like that so I wouldn't think, but it didn't help. I can't help thinking. Something's got to happen. I've got to do something. We only have one more day's worth of bread and peanut butter, and there wouldn't even be that much left if I hadn't opened the can of split pea soup for myself tonight. (It was gross, just like I thought.) We don't have any money, and I can't fool myself that someone from the city isn't going to come to take our house away soon. And Matt—Matt's acting more and more babyish all the time. He really misses Mom and Dad.

I think it's the middle of the night—all our clocks are electric, so I don't really know. But I've got to figure out something before tomorrow. We won't have any candles left tomorrow night, and what are we going to do then? Sit in the dark?

I really, really, really wish Granma were alive to help me now. But she's not.

APRIL 29 AGAIN, REALLY APRIL 30 VERY EARLY

DO read this, Mrs. Dunphrey.

I've thought and thought and thought about all my problems—you'll know what I mean soon—and I decided the best thing I could do would be to give this journal to you, Mrs. Dunphrey, and just have you read the whole thing. I mean it—everything, from start to finish, all the entries I'd marked "Don't read."

The reason I'm doing this is, I realized I have to tell someone about Mom and Dad leaving us. I thought I could take care of everything myself, but I just can't. I'm too tired. I'm too hungry. Maybe I'm too stupid, too. I don't know.

I thought about telling maybe Sandy's or Rochelle's or Chastity's parents—someone like that. But I don't really know them, and Sandy and Rochelle and Chastity don't make them sound like very great people. Then I thought about all those people you'd recommended—one of the counselors or something. But I don't trust them. Really, Mrs. Dunphrey, you're the only adult I could think of who seems even halfway decent.

But the more I thought about it, the more I wondered if

you'd really understand. I mean, no offense, but I was afraid you'd think I made up the whole thing to get out of turning in that research paper. I know I don't have the greatest reputation. And anyhow, I just couldn't figure out how I'd explain everything to you.

Then I thought, everything's in this journal—you'd believe it because you can see I've been handing it in all along, and because, I don't know, I think things make sense the way I've written them down here. More sense than what I could explain in person.

This is due tomorrow—today—anyhow. When I hand it in, I'm going to ask you to read it right away. I know you have a free period after our class. Then I'll come back and talk to you about everything.

I know you'll probably have to tell someone else. But please, can you make sure that Matt and I can stay together? I haven't done very well taking care of him lately—he's sick all the time, and he's wetting the bed sometimes twice a night now. But I'm all he has, since Granma died and Mom and Dad left. And, really, he's all I have.

Another thing—I didn't mean a lot of those bad things I wrote about school. Well, maybe I did, but don't take it personally. It's not your fault school stinks.

And the last thing—don't think too bad of Mom and Dad. They won't have to go to jail or anything for leaving us, will they? I mean, they really screwed up their lives, and Matt's and mine, too, but maybe they didn't mean to. I can kind of see why Dad hits everybody—I hit Sandy that one time. I wanted to hit Matt lots of times when he was whimpering and being a baby. And Mom, I don't know what's wrong with her, but it's like she can't think about anything but Dad. I don't think she's really a bad person.

So, anyhow, here this is.

Can you help me?

Tish,

I feel terrible that all this was happening in your life while I did nothing but nag you about that research paper. All year I've wanted you to break out of that tough shell you wear and dazzle everyone. I never dreamed I should have been worrying about whether you had anything to eat.

I'll be talking to you next period, but I wanted to put this in writing to help you believe me, just as you gave me your journal to help me believe you. I know you haven't been given many reasons to trust adults, but I hope it's not too late for you to start trusting someone now. I intend to be worthy of your trust.

I wish I could promise that everything will be fine now. I can't. But I will try my best to help. You're right that I'll have to tell someone else: the law requires all teachers to report cases of child abuse and neglect to the Department of Children and Family Services. Your parents leaving certainly qualifies as neglect. I already talked to the DCFS about your situation, without using your names. (I don't think it's fair to make the official report without you.) As I understand it, the DCFS generally sends kids in your situation to stay with relatives, family friends, or a foster family. They try to keep siblings together. Ultimately, they will try to reunite you with your parents if that's possible. The man I talked to said you shouldn't worry about them going to jail; the DCFS's focus would be on educating your parents, not punishing them.

I'm afraid you may not want to give the DCFS control over your life, but they will make sure you have food and clothes and everything else you need. You will be free to be a sixteen-year-old, instead of trying to make all those adult decisions for yourself and Matt.

Tish, you did the right thing letting me read this. But you shouldn't feel that you failed in taking care of Matt. You took care of him the best may you knew how; in the end, that meant getting help.

—Mrs. Dunphrey

SEPTEMBER 15

Dear Mrs. Dunphrey,

I almost wrote "don't read this" by your name, just out of habit. But it'd be pretty stupid to send you a letter and not let you read it, right?

Before you get too excited about me writing you, I should let you know this is an assignment. Not for school—it's for this family therapist Matt and Mom and me have to go see every week. (that's right, Mom. I'll explain.) The therapist, Mr. Sarcusi, is always talking about how healthy it is to examine our feelings. He says after everything that happened, I have every reason to feel conflicted. ("Conflicted" is his word, not mine. He says teenagers tend to be conflicted, anyhow. Thanks, Mr. Sarcusi.) So he wanted me to write about myself and pretend I was talking to someone who didn't know my whole life story. Well, I thought that was dumb. I mean, I did that all last year. But I haven't written anything since April, and you keep sending me letters saying, "Please write back" . . . Well, here this is.

Thanks for letting me and Matt sleep on your couch and floor for those three days when the caseworker couldn't find a foster family for both of us. I can't tell you how scared I was when she kept calling and calling and frowning and frowning. When she said, "There are a few more places I could call, but they're not entirely, uh, adequate . . ." I was ready to walk out and just run away with Matt. I was so happy when you said, "Can't I take them home with me?" And I must say, you really stood your ground when she kept glaring at you and telling you it wouldn't be appropriate. Even your husband was pretty cool about things, though I know he was afraid you'd be stuck with us forever.

You know the caseworker decided to send us to the grandparents we never met, Dad's mom and dad in Florida. And you know I didn't think that was such a great idea. I figured, look how he turned out. How could they be any good? And if they didn't want to see us for the past fifteen years, why are they going to want us living with them now? I don't think I would have come if you hadn't talked me into it. (Just to let you know—you were right. The malls are bigger down here. And it's not bad living within walking distance of a beach.) It turns out, Nana and Poppy, my grandparents, aren't too bad either. They're both really little people—tiny and shrunken and old. They remind me of those grandma and grandpa cornhusk dolls that were always for sale every time Village Mall had a craft show. But they don't sit around in rocking chairs or anything. They both go jogging every morning, and Nana asked me if I could show her how to dance like Michael Jackson. (I didn't tell her he's really, really out—it must be hard to stay "with it" when you're seventy-four.)

Nana and Poppy were already pretty old when Dad was born, and they think that's one reason they waited too long to get worried about him. Dad killed the neighbor's dog when he was in grade school, and Poppy and Nana thought, well, that's awful, but it's been a long time since we were kids, maybe that's just what kids do. So then Dad got worse and worse, beating up other kids all the time, getting angry about everything. But he kept fooling them, doing something terrible, then being really charming so they'd think, "Oh, he's all right. He'll outgrow the bad stuff." I asked Nana what they would have done, if they'd known how bad he was going to turn out, and she said she's not really sure.

"Maybe that's why we kept thinking he was okay," she told me. "It's not like today, when all you have to do is turn on the TV and there's some psychologist on some talk show telling you what to do."

Nana says when Dad and Mom got together, they thought he would settle down, but he didn't. And when I was born, they tried coming around, bringing baby presents, volunteering to babysit, giving Dad money until they figured out it wasn't going for diapers and formula. But when the money stopped, Dad said they were just meddling and told them he never wanted to see them again. Dad even punched Poppy in the nose. Then when Nana and Poppy moved to Florida, Dad hung up on them every time they called. So they gave up. Nana keeps apologizing to me, saying they should have tried harder, for my sake and Matt's. She keeps saying, "We can't make up for the past fifteen years, but we're here for you now."

Well, I guess they are. Matt and I both got sick last month, the kind of sick where you throw up about once an hour, and Nana stayed up all night one night taking care of us. Matt's really taken with her, and Poppy, too. He says it's almost like having Granma back. It's not. But it's good to see Matt acting more like a normal little boy. Nana brags about how Matt put on twenty pounds since we got here, and Poppy brags about how Matt learned to fish better than anyone, even the old guys around here who do nothing but sit in their boats all day long. Personally, I think they're overdoing the proud grandparent bit. But when I told Mr. Sarcusi that, he jumped down my throat and told me I was jealous that Matt's doing better with Nana and Poppy than he did with just me. I'm not. I just don't see what the big deal is about gaining weight and fishing.

Nana and Poppy treat Mom like a little kid, too, but then that's pretty much how she acts. She's been here almost as long as Matt and me. When that caseworker from back home tracked her down in California, Dad had already left her for—get this—some nineteen-year-old. That postcard she sent me and Matt was all a lie. She told me she thought we'd feel better if we thought she and Dad were happy together, and she didn't want us to worry that she just didn't have enough money to come back home. Did I ever mention Mom's borderline crazy? I think she agreed to move down here with Matt and me and Nana and Poppy just because we're all connected to Dad. Mr. Sarcusi keeps finding new labels to put on her. He says she's obsessive, delusional, and a long-term victim of the battered-wife syndrome. "She may seem selfish to you," he keeps telling me, "but you need to be more understanding of someone suffering such grave mental illness."

I don't know sometimes Mr. Sarcusi makes sense—and I have to admit, Mom is starting to act a little more normal lately. But I think all those labels are just words. When I try to figure out what's really wrong with Mom, I keep remembering something she told me a few weeks ago. She had made meat loaf—she never cooked back home—and it was actually pretty good. When we were doing the dishes afterward, I made some crack about how Granma would be proud Mom remembered her meatloaf recipe. Mom burst into tears, right over the sinkful of suds.

"I'm sorry, I'm sorry," I said. "Do you want me to say Granma wouldn't be proud of you?"

Instead of just crying and ignoring me like she used to, Mom started telling me a story. I guess when she was a little girl, every morning when she went to school Granma used to say the same thing she always said to me, "Make me proud." Except, where that made me feel good, it made Mom feel terrible. She knew that she could never do well enough to make Granma proud, so hearing those words every day made her feel worse and worse. The only thing Mom was ever proud of was having someone as good-looking as my dad want to date her. So she tried everything to keep him around.

Sounds twisted to me. But I can kind of see why she did everything she did if that was really what she was thinking. She said Mr. Sarcusi's been making her come up with other things to be proud of—like the fact that she kept her job all those years and managed to support Matt and me mostly by herself. I could say some things about that—like, having Granma's house sure helped, and when I started working, it's not like she ever spent anything on me. But I saw the bills she had to pay. I guess she didn't do too bad.

LATER

I gave this to Mr. Sarcusi to read before I sent it off to you, and he really let me have it.

"I want you to try again," he said. "Did you do this on purpose?"

"What?" I said.

"Write about everyone but yourself?"

I don't know. Maybe I did. It's a lot easier for me to look at Mom and say she's getting better, or look at Matt and say he's acting more normal, than to make sense of anything about myself. It's not like I was all flipped out like they were, so I don't have to change like they do.

Except, I can see sometimes how Mom and Dad got my mind all messed up, too. Like, I'll see a cute guy on the beach, and I think, now, there's someone I wouldn't mind dating. But then I think, forget it. Men are jerks. Sometimes I wonder what kind of person I'd be if Granma had raised me without Mom and Dad even around. Or if I'd lived with Nana and Poppy all my life. Or if I'd had your basic, ordinary parents, not the prizefighting crazies I got. I'd be different, I bet. Maybe I'd even live up to that precious "academic potential" you were always talking about, instead of slogging through summer school just to get to junior year.

But it's stupid to think about what might have been. What happened, happened. And I'm not always sure I'm happier now than I used to be. Sometimes I actually miss the way things were last spring. I was hungry all the time, I was going crazy worrying about money and I was scared to death someone would find out Mom was gone. But it's like I was grown up. I was in charge. Here, Nana and Poppy don't let me watch TV until I've done my homework, they write out a weekly list of chores for me to do, they don't let me go to the mall unless I tell them when I'm going to be back—and God help me if I'm not back on time. Come to think of it, they treat me like I'm not much older than Matt. Nana says, "We're just setting limits because we love you." Whatever. It's still a pain.

I can see you, Mrs. Dunphrey, scrunching up your face in that I'm-worried-about-you look you always gave me, especially when Matt and I were staying with you. You probably think I might run away or something.

But don't worry. I remember the bad stuff from last spring, too. I am going to get some kind of job, though, so I've got some money of my own again. (You wouldn't believe how many "Help Wanted" signs there are down here. Everybody's hiring. I can be picky now—no more Burger Boys!) School's okay here. I've made some friends. There are lots of new people, so it's not like I stick out—except the styles are really different here. Nobody has big hair—it's all straight and long, boys' and girls'. Weird.

Anyhow, thanks for the yarn and notebook you sent last week. I don't really see myself wanting to crochet down here. I guess that's a good sign. Maybe I'll go back to keeping a journal, like you wanted. Maybe not. But I am hanging on to the old one I wrote for you. I put it in the back of my new closet, right under my old tennis shoes and that stupid orange afghan.

—Tish

The Always War
by Margaret Peterson Haddix

For as long as Tessa can remember, her country has been at war. When local golden boy Gideon Thrall is awarded a medal for courage, it's a rare bright spot for everyone in Tessa's town—until Gideon refuses the award, claims he was a coward, and runs away. Tessa is bewildered, and can't help but follow Gideon to find out the truth. But Tessa is in for more than she bargained for. Before she knows it, she has stowed away on a rogue airplane and is headed for enemy territory. But all that pales when she discovers a shocking truth that rocks the foundation of everything she's ever believed—a truth that will change the world. But is Tessa strong enough to bring it into the light?

Available now from Simon & Schuster

Others are worth killing for.

EBOOK EDITION ALSO AVAILABLE

from SIMON & SCHUSTER BFYR

TEEN.SimonandSchuster.com

SIMON & SCHUSTER BFYR

TEEN.SimonandSchuster.com

Cara agreed to help Zoe hide out—
no questions asked.
Isn't that what best friends are for?

Elizabeth Woods's debut novel, *Choker*, will change everything you thought you knew about friendship. Learn more at **ElizabethWoodsBooks.com.**

EBOOK EDITION ALSO AVAILABLE

SIMON & SCHUSTER BFYR

TEEN.SimonandSchuster.com